His Little Pyro

A Forbidden Love Affair Series: Book Two

(A love conquers all, revenge daddy romance)

Copyright

This book is a work of fiction. Names, characters, places, and incidents are either products of the author's imagination or are used fictitiously. Any resemblance to actual persons, living or dead, business establishments, events, or locales is entirely coincidental. The author makes no claims to but instead acknowledges the trademarked status and trademark owners of the following marks mentioned in this work of fiction.

Editor:

Cover Design: V. Kelly Author

Cover Art License: Deposit Photos

Printed in the United States of America

First Edition: March 27, 2020

Library of Congress Cataloging-In-Publication Data has been applied for

Kelly, V

His Little Pyro–1st Edition

ISBN-13: 9798615401473

Dedication

This book is dedicated to anyone that feels like they have no one to lean on.

Even in times of despair and loneliness, there will always be someone out there willing to hold you and get you through the rough times. Don't give up, and make sure you keep your eyes open, because sometimes the person you need could be standing right next to you.

A Note to My Readers

Thank you so much for being a part of the V. Kelly family. Some of you were a little disappointed with the first book in this series, *His Little Cheater*.

When I wrote that book, I wanted to write something out of my comfort zone and unlike any book out there. The controversial ending didn't pan out well in reviews and although I stick by my story and how I ended it, I want to make sure that my readers know that this book does have a traditional (HEA) happily ever after, as will the rest of the books in the *A Forbidden Love Affair* series.

In my opinion *His Little Cheater* did have a HEA, just not in the way most people expect. *His Little Pyro* is completely different from the first book, and I really love Amelia and Ryker's dynamic together. It was a fun book to write and puts a cute little spin on the "Daddy Romances" and "Older man younger woman" books out in the market today.

I hope you enjoy Amelia and Ryker's story. Their love affair is filled with passion, fire, dedication, unrequited love, and a deep soul connection that bridges all generation gaps, because love can conquer anything, even if the fire that brings people together also tears them apart.

Synopsis

I'm walking a thin line between revenge and insanity here.

I gave my boyfriend the last three years of my life, only to find out that he's been banging my best friend Haysleigh behind my back for at least two of them. I'm mad at him. I'm furious with her. Men will come and go, but best friends are supposed to be forever. Haysleigh crossed a line I would never cross, and now that she has, it's time to even the score. I have to get my revenge.

But, there's only one thing that I know of that will hurt Haysleigh as much as she hurt me . . . I need to seduce the only man in her life that she has ever really loved. It's the man that I've been obsessed with since I started realizing boys were a thing. The man I fantasized about taking my virginity, even though I knew he couldn't. The man who has always been off limits but has always held a special place in my heart. The man who I have feelings for that I can no longer ignore.

He's sexy.

He's a firefighter.

He's also her dad . . .

That's right, I'm gonna seduce my best friend's dad. My only problem . . . I'm going to have to start a fire to do it.

Prequel

Before the Fire

Chapter One

Amelia

I've got this thing about dates. I remember them—I remember everything. I can remember the exact day that I met my best friend Haysleigh. It was December 7, 2003; I was only five back then, but it was the day before my sixth birthday, and I was having a hard time because it was the first birthday I would spend without my dad. He died of a heart attack earlier in the year.

Everything changed that year for me. Losing my dad meant we had to leave our house in New York and move across country. My mom packed up all our stuff and moved us to a small town in Illinois to be near my grandparents.

I had a hard time making friends. I was shy and the new girl which made me even more of an outcast than I already felt. I spent most of that year alone. Nobody tried to talk to me, nobody even looked at me really. My mom told me that the kids would warm up to me, but they never did. I think my shyness scared them off.

The day I met Haysleigh happened to be her first day of school. She had just moved to town from Chicago and she found me hiding behind a tree crying while the other kids played on the playground.

"Why are you crying?" she asked.

"Tomorrow is my birthday," I sniffed.

"Birthdays are fun. No need to cry."

"My daddy died," I whispered. "He won't be here for my birthday."

Haysleigh looked at me kind of funny and then smiled. It wasn't very toothy because she was missing one of her front teeth, but it was friendly, and at the time, I desperately needed a friend.

"I don't have a mommy. She's been gone since I was a baby."

"Oh, is she dead?"

"I don't think so. My daddy doesn't talk about her much. He says I don't need a mommy because he loves me so much that his love is all I'll ever need. I'd give anything for a mommy hug, though."

"Daddy hugs are the best," I whimpered, remembering how much I loved my dad's hugs and how I would never feel one again.

"All I ever get is daddy hugs, at least you know what a mommy hug feels like. Hey, wanna be my best friend? I'm Haysleigh."

She stuck out her hand.

"Yes, I think I do," I told her, shaking her hand. "I've never had a friend before. I'm Amelia."

"That's a really long name. I'm gonna call you Mia, okay?"

"Okay."

"Here, I was saving these, but since it's your birthday tomorrow, you can have one." She offered me some chocolate chip cookies she had stuffed in her pocket. They had some lint on them, but I brushed it off and ate them anyway.

V. Kelly

I decided that she was going to be my best friend from that day forward and took her chocolate chip cookie olive branch without reluctance. It's weird how friendships can develop over the most random things. When people ask us how we met, I always tell them that Haysleigh bought my affection with chocolate chip cookies and a shit ton of abandonment issues. Most people look at us weird when we both start hysterically laughing over the memory, but we shrug it off as another quirky additive to our relationship.

To this day, chocolate chip cookies will always be the quickest way to win my heart.

Haysleigh and I have been friends now for sixteen years. I don't think I can picture my life without her—especially now that my mother is gone, and I have no one else to lean on but her.

That's why dates are kinda my thing. They mean a lot to me. I connect dates with specific times in my life where something monumental has happened. Which is why I know that today is day one-thousand and ninety-five of my three-year relationship with Willis. He's my uber sweet boyfriend that I've been with since my freshmen year of college. Other than Haysleigh, Willis has been my rock these past few years. I can't wait to get off work and celebrate our anniversary together.

I've looked at the clock about thirty times since I arrived at work this morning. It's Thursday—Thursdays always seem to run longer than any other day of the week. I guess it's because Thursday's aren't exactly a milestone. Monday's are the dreaded start of the week, Wednesdays are the humpity-hump days, and Fridays are the start of the weekend. Poor Tuesday and Thursday are like the black sheep of the work week.

I wasn't even supposed to work today, but I picked up a few extra shifts so I could buy Willis the expensive briefcase he's been wanting. The briefcase is worth more than my last five paychecks combined, but it will be so worth the money when I see him walk out the front door in his cute little suit when he leaves for his interview Monday morning. He's hoping to score a job at a prestigious law firm as a legal intern.

He's currently going to law school, but he still has a few more years before he graduates and takes his Bar exam. He thinks being a legal intern will help him get his foot in the door, that's why he needs this briefcase.

My co-worker June tells me that I am out of my mind for buying him such an expensive gift, because she suspects that Willis has been cheating on me. Her reasoning: No guy can be THAT perfect, and be faithful, too.

I don't care what she says; Willis would never cheat on me. He loves me too much. Besides, he doesn't have time to cheat on me. I spend fifty percent of my day with him. We've been living together for the past two and half years. When I'm at work, he's in school. Every day I come home to him standing shirtless in our kitchen with a cup of hot tea in his hand that he made especially for me. Would a cheating guy do that if he just got done banging another chick? I don't think so.

He's absolutely not cheating on me!

What can I say? I picked a good one. He's thoughtful, kind, and incredibly good in the sack. I definitely have a keeper on my hands, and if my "spidey" senses are working correctly, I have this wonderful feeling that today will be the day he finally pops the question!

V. Kelly

By this time tomorrow, I'll be toting a flashy engagement ring that I can flaunt to every single girl that dares to look at my man with *come-hither* eyes. That's the power of an engagement ring—it's a charmed token that can banish bitches like a fucking wizard in a video game.

I wish my mother had a chance to get to know Willis before she passed away. I bet she would've loved him. Without her here, my life feels empty. If I didn't have Haysleigh and Willis in my life, it would be meaningless, cold, and lonely. I guess I should count Ryker as part of my circle, too. He's been there for me for most of my life and I thank God every day that I can call him part of my family, even though we aren't related by blood.

Ryker is Haysleigh's hot, single dad.

I know this because I've spent a good portion of my life obsessing over his love life. Women have come and gone out of his bedroom, but he never settles down longer than a few months with any of them. I used to joke that it was because he's secretly saving himself to be with me, but that's silly.

Ryker's been more like a dad to me than any man that had ever floated into my mother's love life. I've felt strangely drawn to him since I was a young teen. He was actually the first man I ever had a naughty dream about. It was right after I saw my first erect penis—his penis.

It wasn't the first time that I saw a penis. Bobby Ridger showed me his when I was seven years old. We were playing a friendly game of doctor in my bedroom. My mother walked in just before I was about to touch it. I had no idea what I was doing, nor did he, but my mother was furious and forbade me from ever seeing Bobby Ridger again. He moved away two months later, and I'm convinced my mother had something to do with it.

Bobby's penis was not erect. It was a small little ugly thing that I remember looked like a limp worm. I didn't understand why any boy would want a limp worm between his legs. It wasn't until I saw Haysleigh's dad naked, that I finally discovered what perfection the male anatomy can be. Ryker's dick was a thing of magnificence, like seriously it belongs in a museum or some shit. I can still remember it vividly, like I only saw it yesterday.

I was staying the night at Haysleigh's house. I was fifteen at the time and Ryker had left us home alone for a few hours because he got an emergency call at work that he had to respond to. I should probably mention that Ryker is also sinfully good-looking, completely off-limits, sexy firefighter with the ability to soak any woman's wet dreams with wild, let-me-be-the-helpless-victim-after-I-set-my-own-house-on-fire-just-so-he-can-save-me, fantasies.

I guess that's why I spent most of my night worrying about him. I kept having this nagging feeling that something bad happened to him. All the worrying made me sick to my stomach. I tossed and turned in my sleeping bag all night until the front door opened, and I heard his heavy footsteps walk past Haysleigh's door.

I don't know what compelled me to get out of bed and follow him. All I remember was that I needed to see if he was okay.

I crawled out of my sleeping bag and tiptoed down the hallway towards his bedroom. I was about to peek in the door but then I heard a faucet turn on in the bathroom and the shower door slide open.

It was my unhealthy obsession with Ryker that led me to grip the bathroom door's knob. I wanted to know if he was okay, but I also had this nagging curiosity about what a man looked like naked—specifically Ryker.

I remember the exact thoughts going through my head that night.

Evil Me: *I wonder what he looks like naked.*

Good Me*: No, stupid. you can't open that door. You're fifteen and he's thirty-one. He's like a dad to you.*

Evil Me*: What's the harm in taking a peek? I can say that I had to go to the bathroom . . .*

Good Me: *. . .*

Yeah, I think my Good Me was just as curious as my Evil Me, because that bitch didn't have any kind of comeback. When it came to seeing Ryker naked, every part of me wanted an equal peek.

My hand was dripping with so much sweat that I had to grip the knob with both hands so I could turn it. In the back of my mind, I knew what I was doing was wrong, but my obsession with Ryker ruled out any logic in that moment.

I quietly opened the door, the steam hitting my face in a rushing wave. At first, I couldn't see much, but then there he was in all his naked glory, standing beneath the shower head, with a waterfall of water slipping and sliding down his naked backside. I couldn't move. I could only stand there ogling his muscular ass like a crazy stalker. I knew he had an amazing physique but seeing his butt and all the chiseled muscles that came with it did something to my stomach I couldn't explain. Actually, it made a strange feeling happen somewhere else, somewhere lower, somewhere that never had a feeling like that before.

He moaned. His right hand slapped against the wall, while his other hand started moving very slowly up and down in front of him.

He was masturbating!

I knew what masturbation was, but never experienced it myself.

Young Mia was totally a chicken when it came to masturbation, but had no problems standing in a bathroom watching her best friend's dad get himself off in the shower.

Yeah, my priorities were all fucked up.

*Something like that should've scarred me, but it didn't. I wanted to see more. I wanted to see all of **it**—and yes, when I say all of **it**, I mean his dick. I wanted to see every erected perfect inch of **it**.*

*When he turned slightly toward the bathroom door, I got to see more of **it** than I probably should have.*

I don't know why it intrigued me so much, but I was memorized by him jerking off. I stood in the doorway, watching Ryker as he continued to pleasure himself. I pushed the door open a little more and stood on my tiptoes just so I could see his hands.

Bad Idea.

I lost my balance and tumbled into the bathroom, falling to the ground like an idiot.

"Oh, shit," Ryker yelled. He turned off the water and quickly grabbed the closest towel. He moved so fast that I barely caught

a glimpse of his penis before he covered it up. I swear it was even harder than when I first saw it.

"I ... I ..." My mind couldn't comprehend full sentences. His tan eyes bore into me with so many questions that I felt like I was being interrogated already. He hadn't even opened his mouth and I was ready to spill my guts.

Lie, you idiot!

"I had to go the bathroom," I mumbled, as I tried to get up.

Ryker's huge hand gripped my elbow as he helped me to my feet. The towel barely covered his erection. It tented that terry cloth fabric and almost touched my face when I got up on my knees.

Yeah, my face was that close to his dick. Talk about embarrassing.

I remember thinking to myself, "I'm going to hell for this."

"Are you okay, Amelia?" He was the only person that I allowed to call me that. I wouldn't even let my own mother call me Amelia, and she gave birth to me. To everyone else I was Mia, but for some reason I liked it when Ryker called me Amelia. It made me feel older—more mature. Like it didn't matter that we were sixteen years apart. When I looked into his eyes, I didn't see him staring at me like I was a gangly teenager just starting to fill out her body. He stared at me like I was a grown woman, and that is something I'll never be able to forget.

"I'm fine. I'm sorry. I didn't mean to see . . . you know . . . everything I just saw." My eyes kept glancing down at the towel. His dick never went limp—not once. Trust me, I checked. When he realized where my eyes were looking, he quickly ushered me out of the room.

"You should go," he said it with a tinge of anger in his voice.

"I'm sorry." There were so many thoughts and emotions running through my body that I couldn't think straight. I didn't want him to be mad at me, but he was, and I didn't understand why.

That's when I realized I never wanted Ryker to be mad at me ever again.

"You're fine. Just go to bed. I'll be done with my shower in a minute and you can use the bathroom."

He slammed the door between us. I stood there for a few seconds stunned. I had just crossed a line I should've never crossed. I saw things that I now couldn't unsee, but the funny thing was I didn't want to.

That night, after I used the bathroom, was the first time I touched myself. I couldn't stop thinking about Ryker's naked body and all the naughty things I wished he would do to me. I felt dirty for fantasizing about my best friend's dad, but I couldn't help it. Ryker was unlike any boy in my high school. How could he be? It wasn't like I was dealing with some stupid adolescent boy who liked to push me down, make fun of me, and pull my pigtails. No. I was dealing with a real man. A man covered in the scars and bruises that came with navigating life as an adult.

I swear God must've plucked him from his perfection garden and created him just to tempt all the women in the world.

He sure tempts me. It's like every muscle on that man's body is fit and cut like a fucking diamond, especially his chest and stomach. I still salivate over his six-pack abs like I'm lost in the desert, dying of thirst.

I get lost in his piercing tan eyes, too. The way they sparkle and shine every time he glances my way. I know he's not looking at me because he likes me. He looks at me like he would his own daughter, and that destroys me. It doesn't matter how much I want him; I can't have him. Off limits is off limits, but that doesn't stop me from fantasizing about him.

I should go to hell for all the naughty thoughts I've had about Ryker over the years. It's because of his Godly looks that I achieved my first orgasm. That night after seeing him in the shower, it didn't take me long to reach my climax, because while I was rubbing my clit, I was picturing Ryker's hands on my pussy instead of my own.

It's not like I would act out my fantasies I've had about Haysleigh's dad. Something like that would ruin our friendship forever. We even made up a stupid guidebook that clearly states: *Any boy or man that the other loves is completely off limits to your best friend.*

It's right under the golden rule of our friendship:

I solemnly swear to never let a man come between the friendship I have with my best friend, no matter how good-looking he is or how tempting he may be.

This guidebook has followed our friendship through the darkest of times, including the great boyfriend swap of 2014, when we unknowingly dated Hector Valaquez for two months at the same time. In my defense, I had no idea that Hector even had a girlfriend—let alone that it was Haysleigh. She told me she liked him once, but never talked about it again. Then she said she had a boyfriend but wouldn't tell me who because she thought I'd tell her dad. I thought she was joking—she wasn't.

When he came up to me in my science class and told me all the naughty things that he wanted to do to me and my "beakers" I couldn't resist accepting his request for a date. Not that it was much of one. We ended up in the back of his Pinto, where he took my virginity that very night. It's a technicality that I'm not proud to admit, but I wanted to get it over with, because I knew the man who I wanted to take my virginity, never could.

I found out a few weeks later that he had taken Haysleigh's virginity, too. He even bragged around school how he had popped both our cherries within the same week. It turned out that he had been secretly dating Haysleigh for about two weeks before he ever asked me out.

We didn't talk for almost a month after that. After she found out that I screwed Hector, she swore up and down that I did it just to spite her. It's not my fault that she told me she had a boyfriend, but never told me who he was. How was I supposed to know that it was the same guy I had been crushing on for two full semesters? Had I known that he was already dating Haysleigh, I would've never gone out with him in the first place. Just the thought of him using our friendship against us still makes me sick. We vowed never to let a guy come between us again after that.

"You keep staring at the clock, Mia. Do you have somewhere to be?" June asks, as she takes her place behind the counter with me.

"I think the day goes slower when you have something going on after work. Today marks, day one thousand and ninety-five that I've been dating Willis."

"Can't you just say three-years like a normal person?" June jokes.

"It sounds so much better when you actually count out the days. I think he's planning on proposing to me tonight. I'm not

V. Kelly

sure why, but I know something amazing is going to happen today."

June frowns. She has that look again; it's the *"he's cheating on you"* look she always gives me when I talk about my boyfriend.

"What? I know that look," I exclaim while pointing at her face. "You give me this same look every time I bring up Willis."

June turns away from me and starts busying herself with cleaning off the counter. "It's nothing," she quickly mumbles, "I'm glad that you're happy."

I don't know how, but I can tell she's keeping something from me. "June, what aren't you telling me?"

June whips around to face me. "Look, I know you love the guy and all, and I'm not sure exactly how to tell you this. You know me, all I want is for you to be happy, but I have to tell you this so that you won't get hurt. Mia, I saw your boyfriend sucking face with some girl at the mall last week. I'm not sure who she is, but I've seen your boyfriend enough times to know that it was him. HE'S CHEATING ON YOU!" she screams at me.

Chapter Two

Amelia

"I don't believe you," I tell her, tears threatening my eyes. Just the thought of Willis cheating on me makes my whole world implode. He's my other half; I count on him for almost everything. He's the only guy I've ever loved, if you don't count the super-secret unhealthy obsession that I have with Haysleigh's dad.

June drops a friendly hand on my shoulder, "Where is your boyfriend supposed to be right now?"

"At school," I tell her confidently.

"Are you two linked on a cell phone plan?" she questions.

"Well, yeah, he's under my account."

"Good. There's this app, it's called *Family Tracker*. It uses GPS to pinpoint the exact location of anyone on your mobile phone plan. If he's at school, it will show you that he's there, but my guess is that if he's cheating on you, he does it while you're at work. That's when I saw him at the mall. It was on my day off and you were opening that day. Guys are bastards, Mia. Your perfect boyfriend is a perfect bastard."

I'm reluctant to pull out my phone and download the app she's telling me about. Part of me wants to believe that Willis is as perfect as I've made him out to be. The other part of me has this nagging suspicion that what June's saying could be true.

V. Kelly

For the last few years, Willis has been acting strangely. He put a password on his cell phone so I can't get into it anymore. He did it after I started questioning him about the strange phone calls and texts he had been getting at all hours of the night. He says it's a friend who's been going through a bad breakup, but then the texts have become more frequent. I'm starting to wonder how honest Willis is being with me. He's never tried hiding things from me before, but it seems like he's always trying to hide things from me lately.

If Willis is cheating on me, there's no telling what I'll do.

"Download the app. If he's at school like you say he is, I'll shut up."

"Why are you pushing this?"

June shrugs her shoulders.

"What else are you not telling me, June?"

I throw her my famous Mia glare, and she groans.

"Ugh, don't look at me like that."

When I don't stop glaring at her she sighs. "Fine, I'll tell you, but swear to me that you won't freak out."

"I promise I won't freak out."

She grabs the sugar packets from under the counter and starts to stuff them into empty sugar holders. It takes her two whole minutes before she opens her mouth again.

"I saw a strange car in your driveway as I was driving to work today. No, that's a lie. I see that car in your driveway every damn day I drive to work. It's the same car and always there at the same time every day, and only on the days that you open the store."

"That's preposterous. Willis would never cheat on me. Maybe you saw his car."

"I've seen his car. He drives a black Porsche, right?"

I nod my head. "His father got it for him for his sixteenth birthday."

"Yeah, this car was not a Porsche. It was a super tiny white car."

Instant pain twists in my stomach. That car definitely does not belong to Willis', but if it's the car I'm thinking about, my life just got severely complicated.

I whip out my phone and immediately download the Family Tracker app. After it's done downloading, I stare at it for what seems like eons.

"Mia, are you going to track his phone or what?" June pushes.

"I don't know. This seems very intrusive."

"Intrusive? Your boyfriend is marinating his sausage in some other bitch's vagina juices, if that's not intrusive, I don't know what is."

I can't help laughing. June is one step away from being a professional comedian. She can always make me laugh when I don't want to, "Well, when you put it that way."

There's no more stalling. If what June's saying is true, then I need to know now before this pit in my stomach gets any worse.

I plug in Willis's phone number and hit track. It takes four whole seconds to locate him. The app says he's at our house, just like June said.

Fuck my life.

"June, I need to leave work. I'm suddenly feeling very ill."

June smiles, "I got you covered, Mia. At least we aren't busy today."

"Thanks, June, and thank you for telling me the truth about Willis. I don't know what I would do without you."

V. Kelly

"You'd be serving vanilla lattes to angry customers who get pissed off because you spelled their name with an E at the end of their name instead of a T."

"One time! I get the person's name wrong one time, and you still won't let me live it down."

June laughs, "Only because I've never gotten a name wrong. It's fun to poke at you about it. Now get out of here. You have a boyfriend to catch cheating."

Chapter Three

Amelia

The minute I get behind the wheel of my car, my stomach starts twisting again.

Do I really want to pop this enormous fictitious bubble I've created about my *perfect* relationship with Willis?

The entire drive I play out different scenarios in my mind. The first scenario involves me going to prison. I already see the scenario in my head. I open the door and catch Willis fucking whatever bitch he's cheating on me with, then get sent to prison for murder after I headshot both their cheating asses with a pistol. There's gonna be a chick in prison, I imagine her name will be something like Big Bad Bertha. She's a big woman with an angry scowl that's going to take a liking to me and decide she wants me to be her fresh prison bitch. This is when I end up in solitary confinement because I sent BBB to the infirmary after I stabbed that bitch in the eye with my spork. After that, I become the baddest bitch on the yard, making sure everyone knows that I'll never be anyone's prison bitch!

Ugh, I have a very vivid imagination and have probably watched way too much *Orange is the New Black* lately.

The second scenario running around in my mind is less violent and involves a lot of crying. I'm not much of a crier, but I have a special glitter bath bomb that I've been hoarding for the past two years, I've been saving it for a special occasion—specifically one where I'm overly emotional. When I cry it can get incredibly ugly, and what girl wouldn't want to sparkle after she ugly cries?

This scenario is only a brief glimpse of the aftermath that would happen if I ever found Willis cheating on me. I'd be a sobbing mess, incapable of functioning, and sparkly baths would be the only thing capable of soothing my woes. Even though this sounds like a very plausible reaction to catching my man cheating, my last scenario seems the most likely.

It involves me going full psycho on whatever girl is banging my boyfriend, watching the hoe leave my house in a naked frenzy, and Willis dropping to his knees begging for my forgiveness.

I was prepping myself for all possible scenarios, but nothing could've prepared me for what I saw when I got home.

I pull into my driveway behind the tiny white car June described to me.

This can't be happening.

Tears are already forming in my eyes as I exit my vehicle. I walk by the car, looking through the window, I grimace when I see the pink butterfly seat covers, floors littered with coffee cups, and a familiar trinket hanging from the rear-view mirror.

I look back at my car and see the same trinket hanging from mine. A way too happy fucking chocolate chip cookie necklace. It's smiling at me—taunting me. Hell, it's probably laughing at me, too. Fuck you, chocolate chip cookie, this is not the time for your fake resin smile.

I take a deep breath and turn back to face the house. If I turn around now, I can pretend this never happened. If I take another step, I'm basically deciding to face what's on the other side of that door, and I don't know if I'm ready for that.

Please don't be her.

Please don't be her.

I juggle with my keys before I finally get my shaking hands to turn the key and open the door. My cat Slinky immediately greets me as I enter, running his fuzzy body across my pants a few times before he takes a seat next to me. It's like he can sense something is wrong, because my cat never greets me when I first get home.

Normally, I would call out, "Hello" to get my boyfriend's attention, but today I am on a mission to catch him in the act.

I tiptoe towards our bedroom, where I hear Willis grunting familiar sexual sounds—sounds I should be the only person hearing.

Fuck my life.

The door is wide open, and I see everything.

Oh my God! Where's the bleach? My poor eyes . . . I can't unsee this.

Willis is standing on the edge of our bed, pounding the shit out of a long-haired brunette who is currently on all fours barking like a dog.

"That's right. Tell me how much you like this doggy-style," Willis shouts, "Bark for me, bitch."

This is beyond degrading. I can't believe this is actually fucking happening right now.

I couldn't see the girl's face, but there is a familiar tattoo of a tiny pink butterfly on her left ass cheek that I know very well.

This is so happening.

V. Kelly

The girl screams before barking again, this time like a tiny Chihuahua. In a tiny, sweet voice she says, "That's it, Daddy; give it to me good."

"Oh, you're getting it good alright. I love how loose your pussy is. I've done a good job working it, haven't I, Baby Girl?"

"So good," the girl swoons.

"I love you, my crazy little slut. Tell me that you love me, too. Tell Willis how much you love his cock, Haysleigh," Willis instructs, pulling her hair so hard it arches her neck until she's looking up at him.

"I love you and your cock, Willis."

"Tell me you're mine and mine only," he says, yanking even harder on her hair.

I'm not sure why I keep watching, but it's like I'm frozen in place and words are sticking to the roof of my mouth like six-month-old taffy.

"Why should I say it, when you can't say it to me? I've had to share you with Mia for over two years, Willis. It's not fair," she whines.

Two years? They've been fucking for two years?

My heart rate increases, and I feel tears pricking the corners of my eyes.

Willis bends over her body so that his lips are near her face.

"You know that's all for show. My heart belongs to you and you only, Honey Bee."

My heart breaks. He called her Honey Bee, that's the nickname he gave me. It's also the final straw that broke this camel's back.

"Are you fucking kidding me?" I scream.

Both Willis and Haysleigh break apart. Willis jumps up, his dick immediately going limp.

"Honey Bee, you're home early."

I'm not even focused on him right now; my eyes are trained on my best friend—or should I say my *ex*-best friend.

"Mia, I can explain."

"Explain what, Haysleigh? How I just caught you sleeping with my boyfriend, or how you admitted that you've been fucking him for the last two years? What the hell is wrong with you? I thought you were my best friend."

"I am your best friend!" she shouts. "I wish I could say that I'm sorry, but we've fallen in love with each other. We didn't mean for this to happen or for you to get hurt . . ."

"Get out!"

"Baby, please. I'm sorry. This didn't mean anything to me. I was just having some fun. You know I could never love her as much as I love you," Willis pleads.

"I said get out!" I scream again.

I look into his brown eyes, remembering how many times he's hovered over me on that bed in the same exact spot where he was fucking Haysleigh.

Betrayal courses through my veins like a current of hot electricity. At any second, I'm going to lose my shit.

"What the hell, Willis?" Haysleigh yells. "You just said you loved me."

"I do. I don't. Fuck, I love you both. I'm sorry. Can't I have you both?" he asks. A huge smile forms on his face making me want to smack the shit out of him. I can tell exactly what he's thinking because his dick is suddenly hard again.

This girl has no plans to be anyone's fucking sister wife.

V. Kelly

"Get the fuck out," I scream. "I don't want to look at either one of you ever again."

Haysleigh doesn't move, but Willis is quick to grab his jeans and underwear.

"Honey Bee, let's talk this out."

"Don't you dare call me that. Not when I just heard you say it to her."

Haysleigh continues staring at me with tears in her eyes. "Mia, please don't be mad at us."

"Bitch, you don't get to cry. You can suck up each of those fucking tears and choke on them. You did this. You fucking betrayed me. Some best friend you turned out to be. Get the fuck out of my house before I do something I'll regret."

"Mia, we need to talk this out. I know I fucked up, but I don't want to lose our friendship over something like this," Haysleigh begs. "What about our golden rule? Remember? The one where we both agreed we would never let a guy come between us? You're being unreasonable here." Haysleigh takes a step toward me.

Deep down in the pits of my stomach, something is boiling. Any second now I'm gonna burst like an angry volcano.

Mia's about to erupt! Everyone stand back.

On my dresser is an antique hairbrush my grandmother gave me before she died. My fingers wrap around it, curling until my nails start digging into my palms.

"Get out! Get out. Get out. Get out," I shriek.

"Mia, please. Talk to me . . ." Haysleigh begs, but this time I answer her by hurling my antique brush straight at her forehead. She ducks just before it would've hit her.

"I think we should leave, Haysleigh. Mia seems upset," Willis comments.

"Upset? Upset! You really think I'm upset, Willis? I'm far from upset. Fuck me for thinking that today would be special. Three years . . . three fucking years we've been together, and my present on our three-year anniversary is me walking in on you fucking my best friend. I was expecting you to propose to me today, not this shit. If you think I'm just upset, you're a fucking dumbass. I'm beyond upset, I'm fucking livid. I'm about two seconds away from walking into our closet, grabbing your cherished signed baseball bat, and beating the shit out of you with it. So, if you don't want a Louisville Slugger upside your dumb cheating face, I would get the fuck out right now."

This time, neither one of them tries to protest. I can't look at them anymore. I stomp into the bathroom, slamming the door behind me. Scenario two follows directly after. I immediately start sobbing uncontrollably into my sink, allowing it to catch all the tears that won't stop falling from my eyes. I'm breaking apart like a giant monkey bread cake. I couldn't even eat cake right now if I tried. Just thinking about food makes me run over to the toilet and heave all my anger, sorrow, and breakfast into the porcelain bowl.

I can deal with Willis cheating on me. Guys are like flies, they come and go, but best friends . . . well, best friends are supposed to last forever.

There is a small knock on the bathroom door.

"Go away," I cry.

I hear Haysleigh's voice on the other side of the door. "Mia. I'm gonna leave now, but I'll call you later so we can talk this out. I love you. I know that I hurt you and my words won't ever make up for everything I did, but I don't want you to be mad at me."

"I said get out." My voice cracks and I can barely get out the words between my sobs. I grip onto the toilet for support, but even the sturdy porcelain can't hold up my body as it crumbles to the floor.

Their footsteps are faint as they leave, but my head is so messed up that each step sounds like a fucking wrecking ball slamming into the side of my head. It's hard to catch my breath, my chest tightening with an excruciating pain I can't alleviate. Whoever said heartbreak didn't hurt you physically, has never walked in on their boyfriend fucking their best friend like a dog. The minute the door slams; I curl into a fetal position and continue sobbing.

Betrayal stings worse than anything I've ever felt before. This hurts worse than losing my mom ever did. I was prepared for her death—this I never saw coming.

Chapter Four

Amelia

I wake up a few hours later drenched in my own tears. My bleach-blonde hair is sticking to my wet cheeks like a spider web. My body, weak and wilted by misery and betrayal, can barely move. I find Slinky curled up beside me, he's trying to comfort me, but I don't think his therapeutic fur can cure my woes today.

Was it all a dream?

No. It's all true… everything is true.

My best friend has really been fucking my man for the last two years.

Whore!

Slut!

That fucking backstabbing bitch!

It takes more effort to pull myself up off the ground than I'd like to admit. It's as if every bone in my body has given up working and every nerve inside of me has gone numb. I'm a shell—a shell of a woman who has been betrayed by the two people she loves more than anything in this world.

How could she do this to me?

Why did she do this to me?

I couldn't care less that Willis cheated on me.

Did it hurt? Yes.

Do I want to kill him? Probably.

V. Kelly

Do I have the urge to grab all his shit and start a big huge bonfire in the backyard? Fucking where's the match?

But thinking about my best friend wrapping her pink taco around my boyfriend's tiny sausage, feels like the knife is still digging deep into my spine.

Why did she do this? Willis is a good-looking guy, but no guy is worth ruining sixteen years of friendship over.

I stumble into the hallway and immediately regret it. Remnants of their torrid love affair litter my bedroom floor: tangled sheets of sin, lipstick stained pillows where Haysleigh was screaming Willis's name in ecstasy, and a discarded red bra hanging from my mirror like an angry symbol of their infidelity.

It's not the lipstick stained pillows, the tangled sheets or even the red bra hanging from my favorite mirror that's tearing my heart in two. It's seeing the used condoms everywhere. Not one. Not two, but five fucking loaded condoms tied and dropped all over my beautiful hardwood floor like little semen grenades. I can't get Willis to finish once, let alone five times! Now I know why. He's been emptying his tank into my whore-ass best friend like a god damn gas pump.

Disgusting.

Slinky follows me into the bedroom and immediately begins pawing at one of the condoms on the floor like it's his favorite crinkle ball.

"Ugh! Don't do that, Slinky. You're going to get a venereal disease. Shit! What if I have a venereal disease? I'm going to have to get checked out by a doctor immediately."

My cat looks at me like I just turned into some weird Hydra monster, before deciding that the used condom isn't a fun toy and walks out of the room with his tail high in the air like he didn't just play soccer with Willis' discarded baby makers.

Just the thought of Willis cheating on me has my skin crawling. It's like I already feel covered in scabies, crabs, and every other gnarly sexually transmitted disease I don't want to imagine.

I've only been with four guys sexually, and I don't really count Jimmy Johnson because he was a one pump chump that couldn't last more than five seconds at a college sorority party. I know I'm clean, but Haysleigh has very cavalier bedroom habits, and there's no telling what she's picked up during her numerous sexual exploits.

I stare at my room, my chest tightening all over again. Where do I even start? How do I clean this up without breaking apart all over again?

My phone rings, it's Haysleigh's ring tone. I gave her the ring tone as a joke, but the song *Crazy Bitch* by Buck Cherry has never been more fitting than at this moment. I let it ring a few times, allowing the words of the song soak into my brain. It gets unbearable after a few seconds. I don't know why I answer the phone, but I do.

"Are you okay?" she asks before I even have a chance to say hello.

"You're kidding me, right? Did you seriously just ask me if I'm okay? Of course, I'm not okay, bitch. I just caught you fucking my boyfriend in my own fucking bed. I knew you were a slut, but damn Haysleigh, I had no idea you were whoring it up with my boyfriend like a big, fat slutapotamus."

"I guess, I deserve that."

"You deserve to be kicked in the twat. That's what you deserve."

"Mia, don't you think you're being a little mean and over dramatic? I know I fucked up and all, but name calling is a little childish, don't you think? We're both adults here, maybe it's time you start acting like one."

"Seriously? You're calling me mean and childish? What the hell did I ever do to you that would cause you to stab me in the back like this, Haysleigh? Best friends don't fuck each other's boyfriends."

There is a long sigh on the other side of the phone, "If I have to answer that, then you're more naïve than I thought."

"Excuse me?"

"Stop acting like you're so perfect, Mia. Don't you remember Hector? You knew that he and I were together, and you still parted your legs for him like he was fucking Moses or something."

My jaw drops.

"Wait, let me get this straight. You fucked my boyfriend because I accidentally slept with a guy you liked back in high school? Now who's being childish?"

"You knew we were together, Mia. I told you I was dating someone. I told you I liked him. Yet, you still went out with him and gave him your virginity. I've been waiting so long to get my revenge for that, but you never dated anyone. It's not my fault that it took you three years to find someone special—so special that I happened to fall in love with him, too."

"You're sick. What kind of deranged person waits that long to get back at someone? I would never do that to you, not knowingly. I'm sorry I accidentally fucked the guy you liked back in high school, but I would've never slept with Hector had I known you were together. Telling me that you have a boyfriend but not telling me who it is, isn't the same thing as purposely sleeping with someone for two years that you know I'm in love with."

"Then why are you angry with me and not him?" Her condescending tone makes me want to reach my hand through the phone and rip her fucking throat out. I'm not a violent person, but for some reason she's bringing out the worst in me.

"I am angry with him! I'm furious with you! You're supposed to be my best friend. Best friends don't fuck each other's boyfriends," I scream.

There's a long pause before she speaks again. "Look, I just called to see if you were okay. I'm sorry I hurt you, but I'm not going to apologize for what I did. Sure, it started out as a revenge act, but it turned into so much more. I was going to tell you after the first few months I slept with Willis, but then I realized that I liked him, too. If you broke up with him, then there would be no way for me to be with him and still be your friend. That's why I've let it go on for this long. I'm in love with him, and right now I don't care if you hate me for it. I'm not going to apologize for my feelings, and I refuse to hide them anymore."

"I hate you."

It's the only words I can muster, because I'm fighting tears, and my heart has already been tossed around like black confetti.

"Mia . . ."

"Lose my fucking number. If you think about calling me, don't. I'm done, Haysleigh. I'm done with you, I'm done with Willis, and I'm done being the only person in the world that gives a shit about you besides your father. You asked me once why I was your only friend. It's because you're a selfish, spoiled brat that has no concept of what it's like to be a true friend."

"Fuck you, Mia."

"No, *Hay-sleaze*, fuck you."

That's when I hang up on her. She doesn't deserve anymore of my time, but she definitely deserves the new nickname. I can't

V. Kelly

believe she did this to me because of something that happened back in high school.

Her phone call only fuels my thirst for revenge.

I yell out in frustration, my voice echoing through the whole house. "BITCH! SLUT! I HATE HER! I HATE HIM! I . . . I . . ." My body breaks down into a sobbing angry mess.

My actions are violent and filled with a betrayed rage I can't control. I push a vase off the end table in the living room then start throwing anything I can get my hands on into a wall across the room. My mind is a crazy jumbled mess that can't focus on anything. All I keep thinking about is hurting her like she hurt me.

My best friend . . . my boyfriend . . . my best friend and boyfriend together!

The rage building inside me is like a scary inferno ready to destroy everything in its path. I have to do something. There's too much in this house that reminds me of what happened—of what I saw.

I need to get my revenge.

It's time to even the score.

I run to the kitchen, grab my dish-washing gloves, and throw them on. I use them to throw each nasty condom into a large black trash bag along with every piece of clothing Willis owns. Next, I grab the sheets and pillows from off my floor and bed and throw them out the window. I continue this process until my room is stripped of anything that will remind me of Haysleigh or Willis. The only thing remaining is her stupid red bra.

"You are the devil's lingerie, my friend, and the first thing I'm going to burn in my bon voyage bonfire." I fling the offending undergarment out the window.

As I make my way towards the door, I see the present I bought for Willis hiding behind our dresser. I pull it from its hiding place and grimace. "You're going to make some really nice, expensive kindling," I tell the briefcase.

Before going outside, I raid our liquor cabinet and grab Willis's favorite gin, because what better way to start a bonfire than by downing an entire bottle of your ex-boyfriend's gin in the process?

It's dark outside and a little chilly, too.

I'm not a fan of being cold, but right now the rage I'm feeling is warming every inch of my body. I have one thing on my mind—starting a fire and burning every single thing he owns.

I take four giant swigs of the gin bottle and instantly regret it.

"I hate gin," I mumble, before taking three more drinks. I guess when I'm angry even gin is semi-tolerable.

The wind picks up and whips through my hair, almost like it's goading me to keep going. I dump out all of his clothing onto the brick patio and grab the fire lighter from off the barbecue. Then I grab the briefcase and plug in the three-number combination to open it. I thought it was cute when I set it—115, the exact day we met three years ago. Now I'm going to hate that number for the rest of my life.

I lay it open on the ground and grab the red bra, placing it across it.

"I paid six-hundred dollars for you. I probably should try to return you, but I'm going to have more fun watching you burn. FUCK YOU, WILLIS! FUCK YOU AND YOUR LITTLE WHORE, TOO!" I'm shouting it to the heavens as I flick the switch on the lighter. "BURN, BITCH, BURN!"

I place the flame under the pad of the bra, but nothing happens.

V. Kelly

My voice cracks in frustration, "Come on, please burn."

When nothing catches on fire, I decide to grab a can of gasoline from out of the garage and douse everything with it. Immediately, my nose is paralyzed by the obnoxious smell. I probably put too much on, but I know if the fire gets out of hand, a knight in shining yellow and black armor will swoop in with his big ladder truck to save me. It's a very specific knight I want to show up—a specifically hot knight named Ryker to be exact. Just the thought of Haysleigh's dad swooping in to save me only makes me want to light this fire even more.

Wouldn't that piss Haysleigh off if her hot dad saved me?

That's when it hits me.

Ryker!

He's the perfect way for me to enact my revenge on Haysleigh.

He'll show up, sweep me off my feet, and I'll start flirting with him. I know I'm a pretty girl, and even Ryker can't be immune to a gorgeous girl throwing herself at him.

There's no better way to get my revenge on Haysleigh then by sleeping with her dad. Just the thought of seeing that hunky fireman naked again makes my pussy purr. I've always wondered what it would be like to lay beneath him as he pumps his hose inside of me.

Okay, I'll admit, that was a really bad joke, but come on . . . he's a fireman, I can't help myself.

I take a deep breath and flick the fire lighter on again. I stare at the flame for a few seconds before dipping down and placing it underneath Haysleigh's bra.

"This is for you, Haysleigh!"

I wait for something to happen, but nothing does.

Why is this not working?

I try one more time, placing the flame even further into the pile of clothing, focusing on one of Willis' flammable suits. The minute I place the flame against the sleeve the fire ignites, but I wasn't expecting what happens next.

KA POW!

Instant heat engulfs my face as I'm knocked backward by a fiery explosion. I crash to the ground, my right knee taking most of the impact. Instant pain shoots through my body and I watch in horror as the small fire I started turns into a huge ball of flames that's quickly rising high into the air. It catches the awning above my patio on fire and quickly spreads to the roof.

I'm paralyzed to the ground, regretting this decision immediately. I let my anger get the best of me, and now my house—my grandmother's house that I inherited when she died, is going up in flames.

"Oh no, this is not happening!"

What the fuck did I just do?

I finally jump up, but my knee buckles when I stand up. I think the blast messed it up more than I realized. I limp over to the back hose and attempt to turn it on. The water sputters out of the end and I try desperately to tug it over to the fire while trying to suppress the pain in my knee. Only, the hose isn't long enough, and it doesn't get anywhere close to the blaze. Before I know what's happening, the entire back of my house has caught on fire.

That's when I realize I left something very important inside.

Slinky.

My cat is still inside the house!

There's nothing more sobering than realizing you're about to lose the only companion you have left in the world. The back door is covered with flames, so there's no way I'd get in through there. The front door is my only option. It's like all the pain in my knee disappears for a few seconds, allowing me to run around the house to my front door without limping.

Locked.

I ram my shoulder into the wood, igniting more pain throughout my body. Somewhere inside is my poor, defenseless cat and if I can't get in he's going to die.

I run over to the front window and try to open it. It's locked, too. I can see Slinky in the living room, he dashes underneath the couch. I also see thick black smoke creeping through the back hallway as the fire eats its way through my house.

"No. No. this can't be happening. What did I do?" I scream.

Near my front door is a small table and two metal chairs. This is where Willis and I used to enjoy having our morning coffee with each other. Now it's a shallow reminder of what a jerk he really is. Without giving it a second thought, I grab one of the patio chairs and start slamming it into the window until it shatters over the top of me.

A huge gust of hot air burns my face as the heat from the house escapes the window. My cat is meowing frantically inside. Smoke fills the room, it's so dense that I can barely make out my furniture inside.

I have to save him, he doesn't have much time left.

I can hear sirens off in the distance. Ryker must be on his way, but he won't get here in time to save Slinky. Saving my cat is up to me.

I smash what is left of the glass and climb onto the small flimsy table using it to balance on so I can jump through the window.

I feel the table wobble beneath my feet and before I fall backward, I hurl myself through the broken pane and do some weird roll thing onto my glass covered floor. Shards of glass imbed into my arms, but I'm so focused on saving my cat that I completely push the pain out of my mind and start scrambling to my feet.

Every fire safety class I've ever had as a child disappears from my memory and instead of dropping to the ground to avoid the smoke; I walk upright, letting it smack me in the face.

The smoke is so thick that I can't see a thing. Within seconds I can't breathe and start choking and coughing. Slinky meows, but it's not as loud as before.

"Slinky," I cough. "Here, kitty, kitty."

I finally can't take the smoke anymore and drop to all fours, crawling over to the couch. I can see my cat underneath it, but he won't come out.

"Come on, Slinky, we need to get out of here."

The cat hisses at me and swipes as I reach under to grab his paws.

"Please, Slinky. I'm sorry. I don't want you to die. I don't want either of us to die."

Outside I can hear the blaring siren from the firetruck as it pulls up in front of my house. The smoke is thicker now. The longer I stay in here, the less likely I will be to get out.

With one last ditch effort, I grab Slinky's front paws and somehow manage to drag him out from his hiding place. I'm coughing like crazy and he's wiggling so much that I'm straining to hold on to him. The moment he feels my grasp lessen, I see the frightened cat bolt from my arms and make a mad dash for the front window.

My head starts to feel fuzzy, and my coughing gets even worse, exiting my body in a barking gasp. I collapse to the floor and weakly crawl toward my cat who suddenly has the speed of a cheetah.

"Slinky, wait," I call out for him.

He doesn't wait.

My cat has zero interest in staying in this burning house with me. His need for salvation trumps all my heroic efforts to save him from the fire. He doesn't care that smoke is filling my lungs and I can barely breathe. All he sees is an exit, and he doesn't hesitate to take it.

With the agility of a puma, my sleek gray kitty jumps out the window without ever looking back.

Some hero he turned out to be.

I attempt to crawl toward the front door, but I'm so weak that I can barely get past Willis' favorite recliner before I can't move anymore.

I'm going to die.

I look back just as the flames enter the living room. They eat up the walls, taking down every picture one by one.

I watch as my favorite picture of Haysleigh and me is quickly engulfed in flames. Seeing the picture disintegrate is the last thing I remember, before everything goes black.

His Little

Pyro

Ryker

Mondays are always our slowest day in the station. Most of the time, I sit in my office throwing tennis balls against my wall waiting for calls. I usually staff the station with fewer people on Monday's. Today I let Hank and Billy get off at three because of how slow we've been. I left them on call just in case, but it's been two weeks since anything major has happened in this town, and our budget can't handle a five-man team for twenty-four hours. All that's left is Leroy, Brandon, Lucius and me.

Leroy knocks on my door, "Hey, Boss, you have a visitor," he informs me.

"Who?"

"Haysleigh, she looks upset."

My heart drops. There's nothing in this world I love more than my daughter. Hearing that she's upset already has my anxiety building.

I stand up just in time to see Haysleigh fly through my door and throw herself into my arms. She's crying hysterically. I motion for Leroy to close the door behind her.

"Honey, what's wrong?"

"I fucked up, Daddy," she cries. "I ruined everything, and now . . . now." She starts sobbing again, mumbling incoherent things into my t-shirt.

"Okay, calm down. Tell me what's going on."

"Do you remember that conversation we had a few years back where I asked if it was okay to like a boy that was with someone else?"

I vaguely remember having this conversation with Haysleigh, but it's been a few years and I don't remember exactly what we discussed at the time.

"I remember talking about it, but it's been a while."

"You told me that sometimes the heart can't control what it wants and that falling in love is complicated. Sometimes, you fall in love with people that are unattainable. You also said that although it's bad to like someone that's with someone else, if I felt like it was true love, I shouldn't hide my feelings because all it will do is cause resentment inside of me; consequences be damned."

I remember that conversation vividly now. I do remember telling all that to Haysleigh, but only because I was talking about myself. For years I have loved a woman that I can't have. I've spent so much time trying to turn off my feelings for her that I've often found myself full of resentment. It's not easy being in love with someone you can't touch. I've done everything I can to cover up my feelings for her—including being with other women. Nothing works.

"Okay, yeah I remember that conversation, vaguely."

Liar. I remember way more than I should.

"Well, I did it, Daddy. I acted on my attraction and made a pass at a guy I wanted. I've been seeing him for over two years. I've never been this happy with someone before, but I messed it up. I chose a guy that was with someone I cared about, and she found out today."

V. Kelly

My stomach starts to twist, because I can already tell where this conversation is going and if she's talking about who I think she's talking about. All hell broke loose today.

"Are you talking about Willis and Amelia?"

Haysleigh nods. "Oh, Daddy! I never meant for her to find out. It started out as a revenge thing because I wanted to get back at her for sleeping with my boyfriend Hector back in high school. When she started dating Willis, I had planned on sleeping with him and telling her about it so that it would break them up. That way she could feel what I felt back then, but then it kept happening. Soon, I started liking him. Eventually, we fell in love."

I pull away from Haysleigh in disgust.

"I taught you better than that, Haysleigh. How could you do that to poor Amelia? Are you that petty? Why would you want to ruin someone's life over something that happened in high school? This is probably the lowest and most revolting thing you've ever done." I love my daughter, but she has the tendency to be a spoiled brat sometimes. Her selfishness is the only thing I don't like about her.

"Daaaddy," she whines, "you're supposed to be on my side. Why do you always defend her? I'm your daughter, not Mia."

Her question makes me pause. I have to tread carefully when it comes to Amelia. If Haysleigh got wind of how I truly feel about her best friend, she'd freak out.

Amelia has always been like a second daughter to me ever since she became Haysleigh's best and only friend back in elementary school.

As she grew up, I started noticing things about her that I shouldn't. Like how she developed a very nice rack around the age of fifteen, a rack that only grew and filled out the more she aged. That was the year she walked in on me taking a cold shower—a shower that was supposed to cover up the disgusting feelings I had every time I looked at her. I thought she'd run out of the room screaming after she found me masturbating, but she just stood there gawking at my cock like she wanted a piece of it.

Yeah, that shit WAS NOT HAPPENING.

Not only was she completely illegal, but I was bordering on pedophilia the more I let her stare at me. I covered myself up, but it was too late. She already saw more of me than she should have.

I try to push the image of Amelia staring at my cock out of mind, but it's like that day will forever be stained in my brain. It's unhealthy—I'm unhealthy. Normal people don't have feeling like this. I'm sixteen years older than her, but for some reason, that hasn't stopped me from being strangely infatuated with my daughter's best friend for most of her life.

When she turned eighteen, I found myself fantasizing about being with her more and more. I managed to push back that urge for most of her teen years, but the moment she became legal, it was hard to ignore my feelings anymore. I'm not sure why I have feelings for Amelia. She may not be my daughter, but her age and friendship with Haysleigh makes it impossible to explore anything beyond the relationship we already have. I've done my best to keep my feelings platonic and act like I'm not secretly wishing to see what she looks like naked every time she walks through my door, but it's not easy—especially when she looks like a blonde venetian goddess sent here just to tempt me.

"Dad? Earth to Dad. Are you even listening to me?" Haysleigh waves frantic arms in front of my face and I blink a few times before acknowledging her.

"Sorry, what did you say?"

V. Kelly

"I asked why you always defend her?" Haysleigh repeats, sticking out a pouting lip.

"I guess, I feel like she's my daughter, too. We are the only people Amelia has left in this world. Ever since her mother died, I feel like it's my job to protect her."

"Well, you don't need to do that now, because we aren't friends anymore."

The thought of never seeing Amelia again has me on the verge of tears. I don't care if she and Haysleigh aren't talking, Amelia is special, and I plan on being there for her until the day I die.

"Haysleigh, I'm sure you two will work things out. Maybe you should give her a call and try to explain your side of the story. Be honest with her."

"Honesty will only make her angrier. Would you want someone to tell you that they revenge fucked your boyfriend and fell in love with them?"

"Probably not, but Haysleigh, what you did was wrong. Can't you see that? You know that Amelia loves Willis, and yet you went and slept with him behind her back just to make her angry. I didn't raise you to be vindictive and spiteful. I'm sorry, but I just don't understand why you did it?"

Haysleigh glares at me, "Dad, she broke girl code. Haven't you ever heard of the expression an eye for an eye? It's in the Bible. She did me wrong, so I did her wrong. It's that simple."

I will never understand women and their girl code. I only have one rule for my friends, and that rule is Haysleigh and Amelia are completely off limits to them. They always question me about why I add Amelia to that rule, but I don't need to explain myself. Amelia is off limits to everyone—even me.

"Just call her and apologize. Amelia is a sweet girl, I'm sure she will forgive you."

"I doubt it. Mia is crazy, and she probably is already plotting on how to get back at me. That's how we work, Dad. Remember the great prank war of 2011? The only reason that stopped is because you threatened us if we didn't call a truce. I don't think she will ever forgive me for this one, and frankly I don't care. I love Willis and I'm not going to apologize for that. He loves me, too. He's confused right now, but he'll figure out that he's meant to be with me once this initial blow up with Mia dies down."

Haysleigh is being unreasonable. My heart hurts for Amelia, because no one deserves to be cheated on, and the fact that he did it with Haysleigh makes that arrow through her heart sting even more. I wish I could hold her and make her feel better, but if I went and consoled her, what would Haysleigh think?

"Just call her. You will feel better after you do."

"Maybe you're right, Daddy. I'll call her as soon as I leave here. Thank you for consoling me. You're the best." She gives me a quick kiss on the cheek and scampers from the room. "Love you."

"I love you, too," I shout after her.

I settle into my chair and admire the photo of Haysleigh and Amelia sitting on my desk. It was taken over a year ago when we all went on a camping trip up North. We try to do it annually around the day Amelia's mother passed away. It's to remind her that even though her mother is gone, there are still people in this world that love her dearly.

I remember being extremely jealous for most of the trip. Amelia brought Willis, and I spent most of my time trying not kill him every time he touched Amelia. I shrugged it off like it was just the dad in me wanting to a kill a boy that was making a move on one of my daughters, but deep down I knew the urge

V. Kelly

had more to do with my feelings for Amelia and less to do with her being like a daughter to me.

Like I said, I'm fucked up in the head when it comes to Amelia.

I hope she and Haysleigh make up soon, because living life without Amelia, is not something that I want to think about. Haysleigh is my daughter and I will do anything for her but giving up Amelia is something I don't think I can ever do—not even for her.

Ryker

The rest of the day seems to go by quickly. It's getting close for me to leave and my twenty-four-hour shift has gone by slower than usual. I start to pack up my office when I hear the emergency siren go off. Since I'm almost off, I decide to ignore it.

"Hey, Boss, there's a huge house fire on the other side of town. There are possible occupants trapped inside and since you are the only certified EMT on duty, it would be great if you could come with us. I know you're almost off, but we could really use the assist right now since we're so short staffed," Leroy informs me.

"Sure. I don't have anything else going on right now. Put a call into Hank and Billy, get them to meet us there."

He nods.

I put down my stuff and grab my cell phone. It's always best to find the quickest route to any scene.

"What's the address?" I ask as I pull up the GPS on my phone.

"1452 N. Maple Street," Leroy relays.

My heart stops. I know that address—I know it very well. That's Amelia's house.

"Boss, are you okay?"

I'm pretty sure all the blood in my body has stopped flowing. My head turns slowly towards Leroy. Every word that flashes in my head sticks to my tongue like glue.

V. Kelly

I take a deep breath, trying to contain the fear, worry, and nerves flowing through me. "No. That's Amelia's house. We need to leave right now."

"Oh, shit. You mean Haysleigh's hot friend?"

I'm too worried about Amelia to correct him. Normally, I wouldn't let any man talk about Amelia that way, but all I can think about is her house being on fire and the anxiety that she may be somewhere inside.

My heart races even faster inside my chest.

I grab the keys to the truck and immediately begin throwing on my fire gear as I run out of the room. Adrenaline fuels each of my steps.

I can't lose her.

After the day Amelia has had, the last thing she needs is to lose her family home.

Please don't be inside.

The guys barely keep up with me as I hop into the truck and slam the door. I have the siren going before we even pull out of the station, that's how desperate I am to get to Amelia.

When the last guy hops into the vehicle, I slam my foot to the floorboards, making the fire truck race out of the station.

I swear I'm driving faster than I ever have before. My foot barely leaves the gas pedal as we make our way across town. My heart's beating so fast it feels like African drums pounding inside my chest.

I blow every damn stop sign and light that we come to. "Boss, slow down," Brandon hollers. I look in the rear-view mirror and see his face go green. With how sharp I'm taking these corners; I don't blame him.

I can't think. Let alone answer him. I know it's crazy to be this reckless, but all I can hear are the same words screaming inside my head.

Please don't be inside.

Please don't be inside.

I don't even bother clearing the roadways as we come to lights or four way stops. I could get fined for that, but at this point, I don't care about anything but getting to Amelia. My guys are screaming at me to slow down, but I can't—not when I know she could be hurt.

I can see the fire from a few blocks away. The smoke is creeping high into the air and the tops of flames are flickering above the rooftops.

Shit. This is bad.

We pull up in front of her house and I slam on the brakes, causing everyone in the vehicle to lurch forward. Our seatbelts are the only thing that keep us from kissing the dashboard.

I jump out of the truck and immediately start running for Amelia's front door.

"Ryker, wait. We need to assess the scene first," Leroy shouts after me.

I've assessed the scene enough. The house is on fire and her car is in the driveway. That means she has to be home.

I notice that her front window has been broken out, and then I see something jump out of it and take off down the street. It's her cat.

At least Slinky is safe.

I move to her front door and try the knob. It's locked. Amelia has a gas stove and if the fire reaches her kitchen, this whole house is going to blow.

V. Kelly

I look through the window and see a body lying on the living room floor not moving. Fire has consumed the back of the house and is slowly inching its way closer to the body.

Amelia!

Without even hesitating, I put a gloved hand on the broken windowpane and heave my gear-clad body through the window.

"What the hell are you doing, Ryker?" Lucius shouts. I'm breaking any training I ever had for this one. It's like my mind has gone blank and nothing else matters but saving her.

Smoke fills every corner of the house; I can barely see through the thick cloud of gray ash. I shield my eyes as a blast of fire rushes my face. It's enough to singe my eyebrows, and I'm temporarily blinded by the flash of light, but it's not enough to deter me from getting to her.

Damn, I forgot to put on my mask.

I move across the house swiftly because time is not on my side. If they don't get the hose hooked up and the fire contained, she's going to lose everything.

I see her limp body near the couch. She's not moving and that's not a good sign.

"Amelia!" I shout.

When she doesn't answer me, I sweep her into my arms and carry her lifeless body over to the front door. The fire is spreading quickly. I can feel it nipping at my heels. My entire backside is heated, and the intensity of the progressing inferno has me worried that neither of us will make it out of here alive. I maneuver her so she's draped over my shoulder and use my free hand to unlock her door.

I carefully grab the knob and turn, knowing that we probably only have a few more seconds before this whole house explodes.

KABAM!

Just as I get her to the safety of the grass, there's a giant explosion inside her house. If there was any hope of saving Amelia's home, that's gone now. All that's left is saving her.

The guys rush past me with the hose, blasting the flames with rushing water as the house turns into an even larger inferno. Billy and Hank drive up and hop out to help them, but Amelia is still not moving and I'm her only hope of living to see tomorrow.

I drop to my knees, tip her chin up, and open her mouth before I touch my lips down on hers. I've wanted to do this for so long, and if I wasn't trying to save her life, I would've enjoyed how soft her lips are; but I can't think about that right now—not when she's about to die.

I pull back and do a few chest compressions, before going back in to breathe more air into her lungs. Her face is covered in black soot, her blonde hair reeking of smoke and ash. Her once fair skin has turned a sickly white blue. She's dying.

"Fucking breathe!" I scream.

I keep going, fluctuating between breathing the air into her lungs and compressing her beautiful chest. I can feel her slipping away from me. Her eyes are closed, and she's lying there with her mouth agape like a dead fish.

My heart can't take watching her die.

"No. Not you—anybody but you. Breathe, Amelia. Breathe for me, baby."

Five minutes tick by.

Time is not my friend and I want to curse myself for not getting here sooner.

She's lifeless and no matter how hard I try, she won't breathe. I want to pound on her chest. I want to suck up all the smoke and shit penetrating her lungs, so she'll breathe again.

V. Kelly

"Boss, let me try," Leroy suggests. "You're going to run out of air."

"No," I cry. "I got this. Come on, Amelia, fucking breathe."

I do five more chest compressions and dip down one last time. The first two breaths do nothing, but on my third and final breath, Amelia's body finally sputters to life.

Amelia

"Forgive me, Father for I have sinned. It's been . . . well, I've never made an actual confession before."

There's a part of me that believed that once a person dies, they stand in front of the gates of Heaven confessing all their sins. All I can imagine is a disgruntle angel looking down on me and telling me I'm not worthy enough to pass through God's pearly white gates because I burned my own house to the ground. Then he'd drop me through a hole in the clouds only to fall thousands of feet, my body turning and hurling towards the ground like a pinwheel. Just before my body would smack into ground, the grass and earth would pull apart to reveal a giant pit of fire and brimstone filled with the dead hands of all my fellow sinners waiting to catch me. I'd be handed down through the pit like Sarah in the *Labyrinth* only to land into the awaiting arms of the devil himself who would want to make me his bride.

I sinned lighting that fire, and I nearly died because of it. It's what I get for wanting revenge.

But I never saw the pearly gates or felt the hands of hell wrap around me. I felt nothing. It was like I was encased in darkness. The longer I stayed in that state, the more my mind went crazy.

"Can anyone hear me?"

Faint whispers from the darkness call out to me begging me to follow them. I try to take a step forward, only my body is immobile. I'm solidified in place, paralyzed by the nothingness that roves around me like a vortex of despair. I'm neither alive nor am I dead, and therefore I'm stuck in this limbo, alone and forgotten.

"Amelia," a familiar voice faintly calls out to me.

It's as if my chest is being pounded with a sledgehammer—the violent rage of desperation shakes my soul as three rough spasms take over my body.

"Fucking breathe," the voice whispers loudly. This time it seems to surround me, like an echo in a faint cave that only gets louder the closer it gets to me. It's still too far away, but I cling to the sound hoping it will somehow help me fight my way through the darkness.

Out of nowhere, a single piece of burning ember floats in front of my face, materializing in the darkness like a firefly. I feel compelled to touch it. My entire body yearns to connect with something other than the darkness surrounding me. For a brief second, I force my hand to break free of its invisible shackles, allowing it to reach out and touch the floating ember. The tips of my fingers barely connect with the roving orange light before I'm pummeled with three more crushing pains to my chest.

Wind whips through me, flinging my hair in every direction as it swirls and curls around me. The wind attacks me, almost as if it's trying to breathe life back into my spirit.

The voice sounds like it's right on top of me now, screaming at me from every direction, but whoever it belongs to is still as invisible as the force holding me still. Emotions start attacking me like vicious tigers, scratching me with their rage, battling for control over my future. I'm consumed with love and heartache. The realization suddenly hitting me that death is on the verge of taking me with him.

I want to live damnit!

"No. Not you—anybody but you. Breathe, Amelia. Breathe for me, baby."

It's like I'm stuck in the middle of a brutal grudge match between life and death. Each deity takes a different swing at me. Death pounds against my chest with the force of a blacksmith hammering an anvil, sucking what is left of my breath from my body. Life swallows me with wind, replenishing my soul with quick bursts of air that try to keep me going.

"Come on, Amelia, fucking breathe."

This time, the voice booms louder than a burst of thunder on a lonely desert plateau.

Ryker! It's Ryker calling out for me.

I can't die. Not when Ryker has come to save me. I need to live so I can see him again—he's all I have left now.

Please, let me live. I don't want to die. Whoever is listening, please take me back to Ryker.

A flash of orange light opens in front of me like a swinging door. It pierces my retinas, burning and stinging my pupils with the heat of an angry firestorm. No longer paralyzed, I cover my eyes trying to shield myself from the blinding light. Smoke infiltrates my nostrils, filling my chest with the oppression of being choked and suffocated by the very thing that tried to take my life.

It hurts—it hurts like hell, but despite the pain that is rapidly depleting my life force, I rush into the light, hoping that it leads me to who my heart and head are screaming to see again—Ryker.

Amelia

I blink.

I blink again.

I'm on my back, looking up at an all-white ceiling. There's a soft surface beneath me, I know it's not grass or a plush carpet I'm lying on—it's a bed. From the white fluorescent lights hovering above me, currently blinding me with their light, I'm guessing it's a hospital bed.

"Good, you're finally awake," a sweet voice says to my left.

It's painful, but I swivel my head in that direction.

There's a beautiful nurse standing by an IV pole checking a fluid bag. She's skinny with long, wavy brown hair. She glances over at me and gives me a toothy smile. It's one of those Colgate smiles with perfect white teeth and full lips that most girls would be jealous of. I'm glad I'm not one of those girls. My mother blessed me with her full lips, and it's a feature I'm proud to carry on in her name. The nurse had one thing going for her that I wish I had. Her eyes are this insane color of blue, an unnatural blue you don't often see. She's definitely pretty—really pretty.

"I'm Jessica, your nurse. I just changed your fluids, Miss Morris. Your father just left to go get something to eat, but he hasn't left your side since you got here."

I open my mouth to speak but a hellacious cough takes over my body. The pain grips my chest and squeezes it like an iron maiden. When I'm finally able to speak, two words fall hoarsely out of my mouth. "My father?"

"Yes. Your father. He's a very handsome man, is he single by any chance?" she asks hopefully.

I stare at her like she's suddenly turned into a monster. "My dad died when I was six-years old," I inform her.

"Oh? But he said he was your father." She looks confused, which is fine because frankly so am I. Who in the hell would say they are my father?

The answer becomes so obvious when *he* enters the room.

Ryker.

His familiar muscular figure pushes through the small doorway. Instantly, the ability to breathe escapes me. It's like this every time I see him. My heart gallops in my chest like a wild steed the moment his tan eyes fall on me. His gaze alone is enough to melt me like a popsicle, but then he grins, igniting a fire deep inside my body that's spreading through me faster than a jet plane streaking across the sky. I try to fight the blush creeping across my cheeks, but it's hard to mask my attraction when he's standing so close to me.

His rough voice invades my body like a lust-driven pirate. "I'm glad you're finally awake, Amelia."

Damn, he's so handsome.

He moves across the room so he can sit next to me, but Jessica stands in his way.

She frowns at him.

"I'm sorry, Sir, but I'm going to have to ask you to leave. Miss Morris just informed me that her father died . . ."

"When she was six," he finishes for her. "Yes, I'm aware."

"It's okay, Jessica. He's not my real father; he's just always been *like* a dad to me. He's actually about the only family I have anymore."

Ryker grimaces.

V. Kelly

"Well, I guess if you two know each other it's okay for you to be in here. Technically, we're only allowed to have family members in here." She lays a hand on Ryker's bicep and I notice her batting her eyelashes at him. It's a little flirtatious, but Ryker doesn't seem to notice her at all. His focus is solely on me.

"She's best friends with my daughter," he informs her, gently removing her hand. "She's been a huge part of my family since she entered my life."

I want to tell him that I want nothing to do with his daughter anymore, but I hold my tongue because I'm enjoying his attention. I'm not going to let my feud with Haysleigh ruin this moment for me.

Jessica looks between us for a few seconds before moving out of his way and leaving the room. Ryker walks over to the chair beside my bed and plops down onto it. A friendly smile toys with his lips as he leans over the bed and takes my hand.

"How are you feeling?"

I stare at his hand in mine; basking in how good it makes me feel. His touch is enough to pacify anyone's anxiety.

"Like I just sucked down a trillion cigarettes."

He chuckles. "You did get a lot of smoke in your lungs."

Flashbacks of the fire start invading my mind. I can't believe I set my own house on fire. Granted, it was an accident and I never meant for the whole house to go up in flames, but it was still *my* stupid mistake that caused everything.

"Is my house gone?" I can't make eye contact with Ryker. I feel too guilty.

He frowns. "Yes. I managed to pull you out of the house right before the fire reached your stove. The minute it got to your gas line it was over. The house exploded, and everything was lost.

"Did Slinky die? I went inside to try to save him, but I don't remember much after smashing my window."

"He's okay. I saw him jump out of your window when I drove up. We can put up signs around town to see if anyone has seen him when you get out of here."

A few tears appear in the corners of my eyes. Regret swarms my body like angry locusts. There's no one else to blame but myself right now. Sure, the affair between my best friend and boyfriend was the catalyst that fed my need for revenge, but I was the stupid one who started a bon voyage bonfire so close to my house.

Where am I gonna go now? I have no house to return to, and all my stuff is gone. I'm homeless.

"Hey now, what's wrong," Ryker asks, wiping away a few stray tears that have leaked from my eyes.

"I'm homeless. I have nowhere to go," I sniff, gripping his hand a little tighter. It feels good to hold him. He's the only peace I have in this chaotic whirlwind of suck swirling around me.

"That's nonsense; you know you can stay with me." He smiles, but instead of making my heart flutter, it makes my guilt even more overwhelming. This is the exact outcome I wanted to come from starting the fire, but my thirst for revenge is running cold in my veins. I lost my grandmother's house because of it.

"I can't ask you to do that. I'll just see if I can stay with June or something."

Ryker shakes his head, his brow furrowed in frustration. "No, *you will* stay with me. I'm not about to let you go hopping from house to house when I'm living alone in a three-bedroom home with an empty spare bedroom. You can stay with me until you get back on your feet."

V. Kelly

"Ryker," my voice breaks. "I don't think I can see her again. She . . ." my voice trails off. I don't think it's a good idea to tell Ryker about what Haysleigh did, even if I'm itching to get her in trouble.

"She slept with Willis. I know."

"You do?"

He hangs his head in shame. "She came running into my office to tell me what she did a couple hours before the fire. I know she feels bad about what happened. Haysleigh is just . . ."

"A shitty, selfish, self-absorbed, slut." I can't stop the barrage of s-words falling from my mouth. The pain of her betrayal still hangs heavy in my heart. I don't think I'll ever be able to forgive her for this.

Ryker's jaw ticks uncomfortably. He drops my hand, his smile hardening into a scornful scowl. "Look, I'm not condoning what Haysleigh did, but I'm also not going to allow you talk about her that way. What she did was wrong. Don't stoop to her level; you're too good for that, Amelia."

Yeah, I'm so good I set my own house on fire so you would come save me. I'm far from good, Ryker. Good people don't try to seduce their best friend's dad for revenge.

"I'm sorry. What they did hurt me."

"I can see that. I'm not asking you to forgive them; I'm just asking you to refrain from talking shit about her in front of me— even if she deserves it." That familiar twinkle returns to his eyes. I savor it, because I love it when he looks at me like this.

"Yeah, that's going to be kind of hard, which is why I need to stay with June."

Ryker takes my hand again. "I'm worried about you, Amelia. The least I can do after everything that has happened, is offer up my home to you. You don't need to stay forever, just until you get back on your feet."

"Haysleigh would never allow it. There's no way she'd let me stay at your house after everything that has happened between us."

"Haysleigh has no say in who does or doesn't stay with me. She doesn't live with me anymore."

It's been two years since Haysleigh last stayed with her father. He helped her move into her own apartment near the college when she was nineteen. I offered for her to stay with me, but she said she didn't want to intrude on my relationship with Willis. Yeah, that bitch did far more than intrude; she fucking stormed my relationship like a four-star general.

"I still don't think it's a good idea. I don't want to ever see Willis or Haysleigh again."

As if on cue, Willis appears in the doorway of my hospital room. He's gripping a bouquet of red roses in his left hand and a box of chocolates in his right. The second he sees that I'm awake he collapses on the ground, breaking into a fit of sobs.

"Mia, my Honey Bee, I'm so sorry." He crawls across the ground towards me. My heart breaks when I see him, but it quickly hardens when I realize that he used that stupid pet name on me again. The same one he used on Haysleigh. He's groveling. I can't believe that bastard actually had the nerve to show up here and try to win me back after everything that I witnessed.

"Go away, Willis. I don't want you here."

"Mia, Mi Amore, please hear me out. I know what I did was wrong, but when I found out that our house was on fire and you were trapped inside, my heart broke into a million pieces. I realize I made a huge mistake. I never loved Haysleigh, she's a slut that I used to make my dick happy. She could never make me feel like you do."

His shit-stain eyes are filled with fake tears, and his long brown hair is a disheveled mess that is in desperate need of a brushing. He's wearing a tight-fitting black shirt, one that I'm not familiar with. He must've borrowed it from a friend because it's covered in pizza stains and wrinkled, which is not Willis' style. I watch his lips tremble. I used to love his sexy mouth and how it made me feel. The slight mustache peeking out over his full lips, and the wiry goatee that he's been trying to grow for three years are what first attracted me to him, but now they gross me out. Why couldn't I see how much of a sleaze-ball he was from the beginning?

For as long as I've known Willis, Mi Amore and Honey Bee have been his go to pet names for me. I used to love it when he called me Mi Amore, knowing it was his clever way of calling me *his love* while using my name at the same time. Now it makes me want to vomit. I also don't think he realizes who's sitting in the chair next to me, because he literally just called Ryker's daughter a slut. It's a highly accurate description of her, but not something I'd call someone in front of their father.

I see Ryker's face go from soft and handsome to enraged within seconds. I know this going to be bad—really bad. A part of me thinks I should stop it before it happens, but Ryker jumps up from his chair and has Willis by the shirt before I can even make a sound. With very little effort, Ryker has my ex-boyfriend off his feet. He's holding him high in the air, his hand fisting his flimsy black shirt to the point of almost strangling him.

"What the hell did you just say about my daughter?" he growls.

Ryker

My blood is boiling. A veil of rage hangs heavy over my eyes; red is the only color I can currently see. I'm like an angry bull ready to kill the matador in the ring. Willis is lucky that I don't slam his ass against the wall for the shit he said. Not only did he call Haysleigh a slut in front of me, but he has the nerve to crawl on the ground and try to beg for Amelia back after what he did to her. That jerk doesn't deserve her. He doesn't deserve any of my girls.

"Ryker, I'm sorry . . . I . . . I didn't mean it like it sounded. I'm so confused right now. I'm in love with both of them and my mouth isn't functioning properly."

"Get out!" Amelia screams. "I don't want you here anymore, Willis," she cries. Tears are streaming down her face. I should break his arms for making her cry like this. "I never want to see you again," she adds.

My grip tightens on Willis' shirt, but it doesn't deter him from opening his big fat mouth again.

"Amelia, Honey Bee, I didn't mean it. I don't even know what I'm saying. You know I love you. I've loved you since the day we met. Don't send me away. When I heard that our house burned down and you were hurt, my heart broke apart. You're my world. It took almost losing you to show me that."

"You mean my house!" she screams. "That was my grandmother's house. You will never call it *home* ever again, you cheating bastard!" Amelia immediately turns over, using her pillow to muffle her cries.

The fury this boy is creating inside me is almost too much to handle. There's a thin line between protection and murder and I'm walking it like I'm on a tight rope wearing stilts. The douche is lucky to be alive right now.

He also should be thankful that the nurse picks this exact moment to walk in and save him.

"I'm sorry, Sir, but you're going to have to put that poor boy down before I call security," she reprimands.

I reluctantly let Willis go, but not before I mentally think of all the things I'm going to have to buy at the hardware store when I leave here.

Garbage bag . . . check.

Rope . . . check.

Hammer and nails for his coffin . . . triple quadruple check.

"Leave," I bark, "before I change my mind and really kill you."

Willis scrambles backward and runs out of the room without any hesitation.

"Fucking pussy," I mumble, returning to my seat next to Amelia.

"Should I ask what that was all about?" the nurse questions me.

"He cheated on her," I say, motioning to Amelia, "with my daughter," I add. "Oh, and he basically said he loves them both. He's a stupid shit."

The nurse smiles at me. It's a very alluring smile on a very pretty face. She doesn't hold a candle to my Amelia, who's currently staring at me like I just rode in on a white horse naked and covered in baby oil. If she doesn't stop staring at me like that, I'm going to end up being her villain instead of her savior.

"It sounds like he deserved a lot more than you holding him up by his shirt," the nurse jokes. "I'm Jessica by the way. I've been taking care of your other daughter." She sticks out her hand and I quickly shake it, making sure I don't make eye contact for too long. Any eye contact that lasts longer than two seconds can be misconstrued as flirtatious, and frankly, I'm not interested.

"He's not my father. He's my ex-best friend's dad." Amelia seethes, she's practically slicing through the nurse's backside like she's in the middle of a game of *Fruit Ninja*.

Nurse Jessica has no idea that Amelia is glaring at her; she's too busy undressing me with her eyes.

Newsflash, nurse Jessica, I'm wearing white briefs. I flash a knowing eye her way, raising an eyebrow to question her perusing eyes.

She immediately blushes and turns back to whatever she walked in here to do. Obviously, it wasn't much because she picks up her pen and puts it down five times before she quickly exits the room all flustered.

I'm used to women undressing me with their eyes. It's a look that's gotten me into trouble quite a few times in the past, but it's also very easy to ignore when I want to.

"Are you okay?" I ask Amelia again when she breathes out obnoxiously.

"Don't you ever get tired of women throwing themselves at your feet?" She asks in annoyance.

"Only on Thursdays," I chuckle.

"Is it Thursday?" She sarcastically asks, with an eye roll that's sexy as hell.

My dick hardens a bit.

V. Kelly

Calm down Ryker, you can't have her. She's completely off limits. I remind myself.

I change the subject. "When you feel a little better, we can go back to your place and see if anything survived the fire. I already parked your car at my place. I noticed your purse was inside. At least you still have some personal items."

"I can't stay with you," she whispers.

"Why the hell not?" I snap.

She looks away, refusing to make eye contact with me. "You wouldn't understand. I appreciate the offer, Ryker, but I can't . . ."

"You can and you will. I'm not taking no for an answer, Amelia. Once you leave here, you're coming home with me. There's nothing you can say that will change my mind about that."

She looks over at me and opens her mouth to say something but quickly closes it. A long, drawn-out sigh follows. "Okay, but only for a few weeks until I figure out what to do next," she relents.

I can't hide the smile forming on my face.

"Good. You weren't going to win this argument, Amelia. Not this time."

She gives me a weak smile before turning her head away from me. "I'm tired," she announces. "I'm going to try to sleep. You can go home if you want. I'll be okay here by myself."

I grab her hand and pull on it until her head flops over to look at me.

The moment her eyes connect with mine, my mouth is moving. "I'm not going anywhere. I'm here until they release you. You can't get rid of me that easily."

She gives me another half-hearted smile, but it slowly turns into a frown. "You're too good to me, Ryker. I don't deserve your pity. I don't deserve anything."

"This is not pity, Amelia. This is what it feels like when someone truly cares for you. You say you don't deserve anything, but I think you deserve the world." I push a single strand of blonde hair away from her face so I can look into her pretty blue eyes. They remind me of a cloudless sky, a serene blue, something peaceful that makes you feel at home.

It's hard to fight the urge to kiss her. My hand grips hers even tighter as I battle with the emotions exploding inside of me. The alpha in me wants to devour those full, pouty lips and make Amelia mine once and for all, but the father in me keeps the beast at bay. He has to. Off limits is off limits, and I'm not about to overstep any of the boundaries I've worked so hard to keep up between us, just to give in to the nagging desire to kiss her— even if it's killing me inside.

"Thank you, Ryker. I still think I don't deserve your kindness, but I'm thankful that you're always there for me when I need you."

She gives my hand a weak squeeze before releasing it and turning over.

I'll always be here for you, Amelia. Whenever you need me, I'll be there.

Amelia

It took the hospital two more days before they finally released me. Ryker, true to his word, barely left my side. The only reason I knew he left me at all is because I'd wake up and he'd be wearing a different outfit in the morning. He was never gone long enough for me to notice he was even missing. He would only leave when he was sure I was asleep. It was comforting to know that I had him by my side, but it also made me feel even guiltier for what I did.

"Ready to go home?" Ryker asks, as he wheels my wheelchair over to his truck.

My stomach turns in knots. The thought of going home with Ryker feels more like a fantasy than a reality, but here I am, climbing into his vehicle, getting ready to head home with him. This is so surreal.

"I guess," I weakly mumble, regret still swarming me like bickering mayflies. I haven't been able to make eye contact with him for longer than thirty seconds since I agreed to stay at his place. A large part of me still wants to get my revenge on Haysleigh for sleeping with my boyfriend, but if I'm going to be a hundred percent honest with myself, the last thing I want to do is hurt Ryker in the process. He doesn't deserve to be a pawn in my dastardly plan to hurt his daughter. I don't care how chiseled his chest is or how much my hands want to rake through his hair. He's perfect and sweet. He doesn't need to be involved in this.

He helps me into the vehicle. I'm hyper aware of how large his hands are and where they are on my body. One of his hands is on the lower part of my back, the other is gripping my wrist gently.

He smells amazing for someone who has spent ninety percent of his time in the hospital with me. I look up into his tan eyes and get lost in them.

"Are you okay?" he questions when he notices me checking him out.

"Yeah, I'm fine. I just wish I hadn't lost my grandmother's house. It's my fault."

The corners of his mouth slightly turn upward, there is a thoughtful yet concerned look on his face. "I know."

"You do?"

He nods. "I'm not gonna lie, you may lose the insurance policy if they find out that the house burned down because you set a bonfire to your ex boyfriend's clothing in the backyard." He buckles my seat belt and walks over to the driver's side of the truck. He climbs into the seat.

"God, you must hate me," I moan, throwing my head in my hands. "All those years you taught us fire safety and I threw it all away with one match, well actually it was one of those long fire lighter things you start barbecues with, but you get what I mean."

I feel his hand settle on my back and start to rub. "Hey now, you know I could never hate you. You and Haysleigh are two of my favorite people."

"You should hate me. What kind of person sets their own house on fire? An awful person. I'm an awful person, Ryker."

"You were hurt. It's normal for someone to do stupid things when they're hurt, but that doesn't make you an awful person. There was probably a different way you could've set the fire, like away from the house or in a trash can, but you can't do anything about it now."

I look up just in time to see him pull into my driveway.

"What are we doing here?" I squeak when my eyes fall on the charred rubble that was once my grandmother's house. It used to be a beautiful one-story home that my grandfather built with his own two hands. Now it was nothing but ash and a burned frame. Police tape covers the perimeter, and there's a huge sign in the front of the house that says dangerous don't enter.

"Sometimes even in the wake of disaster, we can find pieces of hope floating downstream," he remarks, sounding like a fortune cookie.

"What does that even mean?"

"Follow me." He gets out of the truck and walks over to my door. I reluctantly exit when he opens it for me.

He extends his hand and I stare at it before shaking my head.

"You're gonna need my support to get through this, Amelia. Take my hand." He doesn't sound angry, but his voice is stern and commanding.

He won't even let me consider if it's a good idea. He gently takes my hand and starts pulling me closer to the house.

"I can't do this, Ryker. It's way too hard."

"You *can* do this, Amelia, you have to."

He continues dragging me behind him until we're literally standing in what would've been my living room. The minute my shoes settle on the remains of what used to be my carpet, I take in the piles of burned wood and the ashes strewn all around me. It's not long before tears explode from my eyes like busted water guns.

"Why did you bring me here?" I cry. "Are you trying to rub what I did in my face? I already feel bad enough."

Ryker grabs my chin and moves my face so I'm looking him the eyes. The pad of his thumb traces the trail of tears sliding down my face. It's softer than I thought it would be.

"I need you to trust me, Amelia. There's a reason why we are here."

"This is torture," I tell him, not kidding one bit.

He chuckles, "Come on, I promise it won't be bad. I'll have you smiling before we leave." He tugs me even further into the house. "Be careful where you walk, there are a lot of things you could break your ankle on if you step wrong."

He pulls me into the only part of the house still standing—my bedroom. Not that it's really standing at all. The barebones of the house—the sturdy frame my grandfather nailed together himself, is barely erect. The walls are gone, my dresser, which was once a beautiful mahogany color, is now black but somehow still in one piece. My beautiful four post bed has been reduced to a pile of kindling in the middle of the room.

Everything I own is gone. No more clothes in my closet. No more comfy velvet sheets to sleep on. No more boyfriend holding a cup of tea waiting for me to get home. Everything I loved went up in flames the second I walked in on Haysleigh and Willis doing the nasty mambo in my bed. Long before I ever pulled the trigger on that stupid fire lighter.

I feel Ryker squeeze my hand. It's gentle, but it forces me to look up at him. I have to blink away the tears stinging my eyes.

"I told you we would come here to see if anything survived. I know this is hard, but if anything did survive, it probably would be in this bedroom." He gives me a smile that's meant to be warm but comes out completely sexy instead. I can't help admiring him. Ryker was born with a set of impeccably sexy genes.

V. Kelly

I look around the empty room and sigh. "Nothing could've survived this. This is what karma looks like after you burn your ex boyfriend's shit in a bon voyage bonfire in your backyard."

He chuckles and drags me over to my dresser. "You'd be surprised what can survive a fire. He opens a drawer and I gasp. Not only is every pair of my good underwear sitting in there untouched, but my parent's wedding rings, the locket my mother gave me before she died, and their wedding picture are in it as well.

"I can't believe it!" I exclaim, grabbing the picture and holding it to my chest.

"I took the liberty of scouring the place after the fire had smoldered out. I sifted through all the rubble and this is all the stuff I found. I could've brought it home with me, but I wanted you to see that even in the darkest times, there is always something positive to hold on to. I know how much this stuff means to you, Amelia."

"It does," I whimper, wiping away a stray tear. "I thought I lost everything in the fire."

I grab the locket and my parent's rings, clutching them in my fist. Holding onto them again makes me incredibly weak. My knees buckle and I collapse against Ryker, sobbing uncontrollably into his strong, muscled chest.

In that moment I didn't care if he saw me broken. Ryker has seen me in some of my best and worst moments. He's always been there when I needed him, no questions asked. It's like he knows what I need to get me through all the rough times in my life. Standing in the burned corpse of my grandparent's home, knowing I'm the reason it burned to ground, definitely qualifies as a rough time. Maybe even the roughest time I've ever had. Because not only am I standing on the ashes of what used to be my life, but I'm also riding a wave of guilt like a jacked-up surfboard for even thinking about using Ryker for revenge on his daughter.

Fucking him would be a perfect way to get back at Haysleigh., but he doesn't deserve that. Ryker means more to me than he will ever realize. Sure, he's been like a father to me since I was a little girl, but the feelings I have for him go beyond a father/daughter relationship. I think I'm in love with him. It's a love that would be rather incestuous if we were actually related.

Thankfully, the blood that runs through my veins is not connected to any part of his DNA. It does, however, have an even deeper connection to Ryker than phosphates and nucleotides ever could. Because the blood that rushes through my veins drops directly into my heart, and that's exactly where I've stored my secret feelings for him for the past fifteen years.

Now that Haysleigh and I aren't friends anymore, maybe it's time to act on these secret feelings I have for her father. If Haysleigh finds out about it, then great—that will be the best revenge ever, but revenge doesn't really matter to me right now. I'm consumed with curiosity. For the last ten years I've secretly desired him, and now that I'm going to be living with him, I want to explore what my heart has always wanted—Ryker.

Ryker

Amelia walks through my front door hesitantly. She's carrying the remnants of her house in her arms. Not much survived, but what did survive was a handful of sexy panties, her parent's jewelry, a few pictures I saved from the fire and her fire safe that thankfully had all her important documents inside. We also managed to swing by a local thrift store and pick up some cheap clothing for her to wear. She insisted on shopping cheap because thrift stores had the best deals. She also refused my help when I offered to pay for it all. Sure, she only spent fifty dollars, but with everything she just went through, the last thing she needs to worry about is buying new clothing.

"I have to start all over," she mumbles, staring at my living room like it's the first time she's ever been there.

"You can put your stuff in the guest room, Amelia. You're free to stay here as long as you like. All I ask is that you pick up after yourself and help me keep the house clean. I don't plan on charging you rent, but if you can help me keep things going around here, that would be great."

"I don't plan on staying long," she whispers. I'm not sure why she's acting so timid and afraid. It's not like this is the first time she's been in my house. She looks nervously around the room, and then I catch her staring at me with a strange look in her eye. The second she realizes that I'm staring back at her, she frowns and looks away like I've upset her.

"Is something wrong?"

"I don't see how this will work, Ryker. Haysleigh . . . well, we aren't friends anymore. If she comes home and finds me here, it will upset her."

She has a point. My daughter is good at holding grudges, but I didn't raise Haysleigh to be a bitch, and I know she would be thankful that I gave Amelia a place to stay, despite the circumstances that brought her here.

"She'll be fine. Besides, Haysleigh doesn't live here anymore. She may pop in from time to time, but I'm sure she won't try to start anything with you."

She mumbles something that sounds like, "You don't know Haysleigh very well, do you?" before taking another step into the room.

"What was that?" I ask her, knowing very well what she said.

"Nothing," she quickly replies, shooting me a sliver of a smile. I love it when she smiles, even if I can see that her heart isn't really in it right now.

"I have to stop by work and check on the station. Make yourself comfortable, Amelia. This is your home now, for as long as you need it."

I start to walk out the door when I feel her tug my hand. I turn towards her and see her staring at me again.

"Thank you, Ryker. I don't know where I would be if it wasn't for your generosity."

Thinking about what would've happened if I hadn't gotten to her house in time scares me more than I like to admit. What would've happened if I lost her in that fire? What if she hadn't survived? Damn . . . I don't even want to think like that. She's here. She's safe. She's holding my hand and staring up at me with those big round doe eyes that I love so much. I wish she wouldn't look at me like that—the way a woman does when they are about to devour you. I know she doesn't mean it. Amelia only sees me as a father figure, but I can't help feeling that familiar twang of attraction course through my body like a rushing river the longer I stare into her eyes.

She's more beautiful than she will ever realize, and I wish I didn't feel this way when she looks at me. She's supposed to be like a daughter to me, and yet I can't help wondering what she looks like underneath her new thrift store clothes.

I shake my head to remove the thought from my head like I've done so many times before when my mind began to think inappropriate thoughts I shouldn't have about Amelia. Having her live with me won't affect our relationship. I won't let it. Yet, as I look deep into her sky colored eyes, I can't stop my thoughts from roving to that dangerous zone I'm trying so hard to stay away from.

I'm a strong man. I know how to keep my distance. Why is having Amelia stay with me challenging all the strength inside of me?

"Ryker?" she questions. She must've noticed the internal struggle on my pained face.

"Sorry, Amelia. I need to get going. I'll be back later tonight."

I tug my hand out of hers and quickly slink out the door. My dick throbs in my pants with every step I take away from her.

Damn, this definitely is not going to be as easy as I thought.

When I get to work, Leroy is waiting for me. He's holding a tan manila folder in his hands and is leaning against the wall next to the doorway that leads into my office. He's extremely tall, at least three feet taller than I am, with dark mocha skin and a pronounced nose, one could almost call it bulbous because it takes up half his face. His lean body is covered in tattoos, but he's also very muscular. You get all sorts of muscles when you throw around hoses all day.

"Hey, Boss. We were wondering when you would come back. How is Amelia doing?"

I shake my head and open the door so we can both go inside. "She's good. She's going to be staying with me for a few weeks until she gets back on her feet."

Leroy's mouth pulls into a knowing smile. "Is she? Any plans on breaking in your daughter's best friend?"

I glare at him. "No. She's like a daughter to me."

"Well, you have some strong will power then. If a girl who looks like her lived in my house, I'd be banging that pussy every night."

It wasn't like Leroy to be so vulgar when talking to me. He must've noticed my disapproving frown, because he quickly corrects himself.

"Sorry, it's been a long time since I've gotten laid. Plus, I've been working your hours the last few days. I couldn't have a social life right now if I tried. I apologize for what I said. Please don't fire me. I really need this job."

My glare softens to a more piteous gaze. I feel his pain. It's been six long months since I last slept with a woman. I might have to remedy that soon, to cover up the feelings I'm having for Amelia.

"I'm not going to fire you, Leroy, but don't speak to me that way when we're at work. We're friends, but I am your boss. There is a certain hierarchy we need to follow here."

V. Kelly

"Right. I'm sorry, Boss." He stands there a few seconds staring at me, before he realizes that he actually needed to talk to me about something other than getting a piece of ass.

"Oh, here. The insurance company called and wants the report on the fire that happened at Amelia's place. I would've filled it out myself, but I know that this case is important to you."

Leroy hands me the folder and I reluctantly take it from him. Technically, I shouldn't be handling her case at all, that would be a conflict of interest. Some might even call it borderline nepotism, but that would only be the case if she actually was my daughter. Which she's not.

She's definitely NOT my daughter.

"Thanks. I'll look over it right now."

Leroy stands there for a few more awkward seconds before excusing himself and leaving me alone in my office.

Being back at work after two days of being off feels odd. I haven't taken a day off work in a very long time. I'm a die-hard employee. I worked my ass off to become chief of this fire station, and that means sometimes you have to make sacrifices like not having days off. I've even come into work sick as a dog before just to keep the station going when we were short staffed due to a flu epidemic. That takes some commitment. My body felt like it had been run over by a semi-truck for two weeks straight. Luckily, our calls were very minimal, and we didn't have to go out much. Otherwise, I might've infested the whole town with my flu germs.

I plop into my desk chair and let out a long sigh. How am I going to tell Haysleigh about Amelia? I know I raised her to be understanding, but it feels sort of like I'm picking a side and I don't really want to do that.

My phone ringing interrupts my thoughts.

"Fifth street fire station, Chief Thompson speaking."

"Yes, Chief Thompson. This is Cindy Risner from Holtz and Sherman Insurance company. I'm wondering if you had time to look over the Morris file yet?"

Morris is Amelia's last name. My stomach drops.

"Not yet, I have it on my desk to go through right now."

"That's wonderful. The reason I'm calling is because my boss has made it very clear that he believes this fire was intentionally set and therefore Miss Morris foregoes the insurance claim."

"What do you mean by intentionally set?"

"Well, from the reports the County Forensic Scientist sent to us, it looks as though Miss Morris started a fire in her backyard with the intent to burn the house down," she responds dryly.

"Mrs. Risner, I can personally vouch for Miss Morris in stating that the fire was not intentionally set to burn her house down. It was a complete accident."

"The report from the county states that she purposely set clothing and other goods on fire in the backyard. This resulted in the entire property going up in flames. Would that not indicate arson?"

My throat starts to dry out, and my mouth suddenly feels like cotton candy. "It's true that some articles of clothing and other miscellaneous items were found on the back porch and they were what started the fire, but the items in question were placed in a trash can and when she went inside to grab something, the trashcan knocked over and the fire spread to the house."

Shut up, you idiot. Stop lying.

"There was no report of a trashcan being anywhere near the clothing in the Forensic Scientist's report." I hear her shuffle some papers in front of her.

V. Kelly

Shit, I need to fix this now. Maybe she will be a little more sympathetic if I tell her what really happened.

"That's because the trashcan was plastic and melted in the blaze. I'm sorry, but I was the first responder to the scene and spoke directly to Miss Morris myself. Let me ask you something, Cindy. Have you ever been in love?"

The other line goes silent, as if my question has left her speechless.

"Why yes, I have."

"Have you ever been cheated on?"

She scoffs, "I don't think that's any of your business, Chief Thompson or relevant in this conversation."

"You're right, it's not. The reason I ask is because this young woman has been through a very traumatic experience. She caught her boyfriend cheating on her and out of anger burned some items of his that he had left in her house. She made some poor choices like burning the items too close to her house and in a receptacle that wasn't suitable for burning, but she didn't do it with the intent on setting her house on fire. That house belonged to her grandparents and her grandfather built it himself from the ground up. The last thing she wanted was for it to burn to the ground. She put her life on the line to save her cat that was trapped inside and almost died. Now tell me, Cindy, does that sound like someone who purposely wanted her house to catch on fire?"

I can literally feel sweat dripping down my forehead. This is what I get for being off for two days. If I had been here, I could've cleaned up the mess in the backyard before the County ever had a chance to examine the property. Not only is Amelia going to lose her insurance claim, she might also get charged with arson.

"No. It doesn't sound like she intentionally set the house on fire, but it does sound like she is responsible for the destruction of someone else's property and that *is* arson is it not?"

"It is." My mouth ticks in frustration.

"Please make sure that when you send in the final report, that you include what we just discussed. This is useful information for the prosecutor's case. We will be in touch soon, Chief Thompson. I expect that report by tomorrow morning. Thank you for your time." The cold-hearted woman hangs up on me before I even have a chance to respond.

I slam my fists against the cold wood of my desk and growl out in frustration.

"FUUUUUUUCK," I yell.

Leroy comes running into my office.

"Boss, is everything okay?" he asks.

"No, Leroy, everything is not okay, but don't worry about it. I'll take care of it." And I will.

I'm not going to allow Amelia to be prosecuted and convicted of arson. I know she's the one who started the fire, but she didn't do it to be malicious, she did it because she was hurting. Why should she suffer any more than she already has?

Amelia

Being in Ryker's house alone is a little unnerving. I spend my first few hours walking up and down his halls looking at every family picture. There are mostly pictures of Haysleigh hanging up on the walls, but there are a few of Ryker with his shirt off and I find myself running my fingers over each picture, admiring his chiseled face and muscled torso.

For years I've wanted this man, and now I'm literally living under his roof. I absentmindedly walk through his house and find myself in his bedroom.

His bed is neatly made. It's a large king-sized bed with a black down comforter and chic leather headboard. At the foot of his bed is a small bench with shoe storage. I walk over to his closet and run my fingers over his clothing. I grab one of his white button-up shirts and take off my top and bra. Both are itching me like crazy because I put them on directly after we left Goodwill and I haven't washed them yet.

The thought of wearing clothes that haven't even been washed makes my skin crawl. I had no other choice at the time, but it still makes me feel icky. For some reason, I take off my jeans and panties as well. Ryker's shirt is big enough to cover my whole body. It drops just above my thighs, and the sleeves hang well below my wrists. The shirt is gigantic on me but feels good against my skin.

I walk over to his bed and crawl up onto the comforter.

I can't believe Ryker actually sleeps here. I wonder if he sleeps in boxers or nude? Thoughts of that fateful day when I saw him naked in the shower flood my brain and I start moving and wriggling to fight off the urge to touch myself.

My hand squeezes the nipple on one of my breasts while the other navigates the hills of my body until it stops just above my mound. Ryker shouldn't be home for a while, he'd never know if I got myself off on his bed.

My fingers work their way down my slit and slide in, massaging the very top of my clit. I moan in response enjoying the feeling of my fingers while picturing they aren't my own. I wish it was Ryker fingering me instead. His big hands, rough and covered with calluses tease every inch of my body as his fingers flick and massage my clit. Yes, I bet he's really good at teasing women.

I don't usually masturbate so recklessly. I've definitely never masturbated on someone else's bed before, but I can't help myself. This is the closest to Ryker touching me that I'll ever get.

So, I let my imagination run freely.

Ryker's lips touch the inside of my thigh, then his warm hot tongue slides up until it reaches my entrance. I feel it start gliding along my slit, putting pressure on my clit as he rolls and rocks it against his tongue.

It's almost like I can actually feel him touching me. His hands, his tongue. Everything. I feel it all.

An orgasm attacks me, it's strong and wicked. Rocking through every inch of my body until my toes are curling and I can no longer hold in the moans I've been hiding.

"God, Ryker, YES!" I scream.

My entire body shudders in satisfaction, my head swimming in a euphoric dizziness I haven't felt in a while. It would've been

V. Kelly

ten times worse if Ryker had walked through the door and caught me doing it. The naughtiness of masturbating on Ryker's bed makes me feel devious. It gave me a high I can't explain, and I think it's something I might have to do again and again when he's not here. If I can't have Ryker physically, then what's the harm of having a little fun on his bed every day?

I sit up and adjust his shirt. Buttoning a few of the buttons that came loose before reaching down to tug back on my panties.

I carefully pick up my discarded thrift store clothes from off the floor and walk back into the guest bedroom. Ryker could be home any minute. What would've happened if he caught me fingering myself on his bed? Would he have run from the room screaming? Would he have wanted to join me? The thought of Ryker masturbating in front of me only makes me want to play with myself more.

I shake off the urge to pleasure myself a second time and toss the clothing I bought from Goodwill into his washer. Most of the clothing is dark, so I throw it in altogether and start the washing machine.

For a single man living alone, Ryker has a pretty tidy house. There are no dirty clothes lying around anywhere or old pizza boxes sitting on the counters. It's very clean and free of clutter. It's the exact opposite of any man's house I've been in before. Not that I've been in many men's houses. I've only been with four guys in the past, so my experience is highly limited. But I have gone with Willis to some pretty crazy parties at his friend's houses and their homes were an absolute disaster.

I meander out of the laundry room and work my way to the kitchen. Maybe I can prepare a delicious dinner for Ryker to thank him for letting me stay here with him.

He has the typical bachelor foods in his cupboard: Top Ramen, boxed macaroni and cheese, a few boxes of spaghetti, and all the canned food staples. I find a nice loaf of sourdough bread on top of his fridge in a bread basket and decide to make him some homemade spaghetti. I find basically everything I need, even some Italian sausage in his refrigerator that he had been defrosting.

By the time he comes home a few hours later the kitchen smells like an Italian Bistro.

"MMM, something smells amazing in here," he remarks from the garage door. He comes around the corner and stops dead in his tracks when he sees me on my tiptoes trying to reach for a measuring cup on the top shelf.

"Um, Amelia, what are you wearing?" he asks, his voice breaking into a choked whisper.

"Oh, my gosh. I'm so sorry, Ryker. The new clothes I got were itching me like crazy so I kinda invaded your closet and grabbed a shirt. I hope you don't mind. My laundry should be done soon."

He looks at me uncomfortably. Then his eyes wander down my body until they're focused on my long, tan legs.

"You were in my room?"

I feel a nervous blush warm my face. Oh, I was definitely in your room. I was also on your bed, masturbating like a deranged psychopath all over your very nice comforter.

I don't tell him that.

"You told me to make myself at home," I remind him, as if that will make what I did okay.

"Let me get you some pants."

"They won't fit. I tried."

He lifts an eyebrow. "You tried on my pants?"

V. Kelly

My blush deepens.

"Um, yeah. I'm sorry if that wasn't okay."

"It's fine," he whispers, his eyes are now focused on the buttons of the shirt I'm wearing, which I'm now realizing are unbuttoned dangerously low and the shirt is completely see-through. You can see my darkened areolas and my perky nipples through the white fabric, and the hills of my breasts are on display in the open part of the shirt.

I should cover myself up, but I kinda like how he's looking at me.

I take a dangerous step towards him.

He doesn't move.

"Did you have a good day at work?" I ask, taking my hand and toying with the open part of my shirt.

"Not really." He bites his bottom lip. Then he holds it, like it's the only thing he can do to stop himself from doing something he'll regret.

There's a stool on the outside of his kitchen counter. I sit on it, making sure to open my legs, as I stretch back to lean against the counter. He can now see my panties and even more of my breasts.

"What are you doing?" he asks me, as he watches my hand run slowly down my thigh.

"I've been on my feet all day. I need to sit down for a minute."

He somehow has moved closer to me. If he reaches out, he'd be able to touch me.

I want him to touch me.

"How long until your clothes come out of the dryer?"

"Ten minutes," I reply.

He moves even closer to me. I can feel the fabric of his jeans against the sides of my knees. He lurches forward, boxing me in with his strong muscular arms. He moves into the space between my legs, I can feel his dick through his pants, it's hard and pushing against his zipper. His face dips down and I feel his lips rest against my ear as he whispers into it.

"I suggest you put some clothes on before I do something we both will regret."

It's the first time he's ever talked to me this way, and I find it incredibly sexy.

I pull back so I can look into his eyes, my cheek brushes against his, it's rough and covered in stubble.

"What if I don't want to?" I challenge, while a flirtatious smile toys with the corner of my mouth.

He stares into my eyes for a few seconds. There is a dangerous look in them, like at any second he's going to grab my thighs and carry me off to his bedroom.

I suck the corner of my bottom lip into my mouth as I carefully run my fingers up the inside of his pant leg. When they briefly touch the bulge in his jeans, his eyes widen.

This is it. Time to reel him in.

I grab the bulge and squeeze it gently.

He jumps away from me. The dangerous look that was in his eyes seconds ago quickly disappears and is replaced with confusion.

Shit.

"How long until dinner?" he hurriedly asks.

"About twenty minutes give or take."

"Okay, I'm going to go take a shower and get changed. We have some things we need to discuss," he's frowns.

Uh oh, maybe I took things too far.

V. Kelly

"Okay, we'll talk while we eat."

He leaves the room. My eyes trail after him like lost puppies. Why does he have to be so damn good-looking? Damn, I thought his ass looked amazing in jeans, but it looks even better in the khaki dress pants he's wearing.

I was so close.

Whatever he needs to talk to me about sounds serious. I hope my little stunt to seduce him didn't piss him off.

Once I saw the way he was looking at me, I couldn't help myself. I've never seen Ryker look at me that way before and I wanted to know if he was feeling the same way I was.

I probably shouldn't have been wearing his shirt. Not that I minded him catching me wearing it. Although, having Ryker stare at me like that only increases my sexual frustration. I'm going to have to figure out some way to deal with my attraction to Ryker, otherwise it's going to destroy me.

Ryker

I'm going to have to take the coldest shower ever to get rid of this raging hard-on Amelia gave to me.

That was too close. I almost fucked her right there in my kitchen.

Walking in on her reaching into my cupboard as my button-down shirt rode up her backside is a sight I don't want to forget. I'm storing that image in my spank bank arsenal for safe keeping. Her pert little ass in those white cotton panties would make any man's dreams sopping wet, and I got to see them firsthand. Those cotton panties wouldn't stand a chance once my massive hands got a hold of them. One pull and I'd be shredding them like confetti. Damn, my dick gets even harder thinking about all the fucked-up things I could've done to her in that moment.

It was like she was purposely trying to seduce me. The way she sat on that stool with her legs wide open, inviting me in. It would've been so easy to take her. Slide the zipper down, pull my dick out and her panties to the side.

Fuck. I'm even harder now thinking about it.

She can keep my shirt. I always thought it looked great on me, but it looks fucking amazing on her.

Yeah, she can definitely keep my shirt.

I walk into my bedroom and immediately notice that someone's been on my bed. I make it a point every morning to make it. I don't just throw the comforter over rumpled sheets and call it good. I spend at least five minutes of my morning tucking in my sheets making sure they have crisp, clean hospital corners with no wrinkles. My father was in the military, so he taught me and my cousins how to make a bed according to military standards. I even pull my comforter so that it has a nice clean edge. That's why I know that my bed has definitely been disturbed. There is human sized wrinkle dead center of the bed—a person about Amelia's size.

Was Amelia laying on my bed before I got home? The thought of Amelia lying on my bed makes my dick even more uncomfortable in my pants. If I don't relieve myself quick, I'll end up with a major case of blue balls before dinner. I walk across the room and pull the corners of my bed, fixing the wrinkles before making my way to the bathroom.

The cold shower does nothing to alleviate my sexual frustrations. Not only am I picturing Amelia in my button-down shirt and her white panties, but I'm also picturing her lying on my bed pleasuring herself at the same time.

There's something seriously wrong with me. She's literally half my age and I can't stop thinking about her. She's also my daughter's best friend. Well, ex-best friend, but still she's been like a daughter to me for the past fifteen years. I shouldn't be having these impure thoughts about her. But here I am, imagining what it would like to see Amelia outstretched on my bed pleasuring herself. My feelings are deep. I don't want to fuck her. I want to kiss every inch of her perfect little body and whisper those three little words into her ear, while stroking myself in and out of her.

Damn, now I'm gonna have to masturbate to get these images out of my head. It's the only way I'm going to survive her living with me, short of actually acting out these fantasies in real life.

Maybe I can talk to Chase or Scott tomorrow when I meet them at the bar and see if they know of any easy girls that they can hook me up with. The best way to stop thinking about Amelia is to get another girl underneath me stat.

After my cold shower and quick jerk-off . . . because yeah, thinking about making love to Amelia makes me a come faster than usual; I change into something more comfortable and make my way to the dining room where Amelia has conveniently laid out a delicious Italian dinner.

Sourdough bread with garlic butter, a crisp green salad tossed with a light Italian dressing, croutons, and parmesan cheese, and a large helping of fresh spaghetti with homemade meatballs sits in the middle of the table. She set out two place settings, lit a candle, and even turned down the parlor lights to make it a little more romantic. Yeah, having her here is definitely a blessing in disguise. It's been a long time since I've eaten this well—you don't cook much when you're always on call.

I sit at the table, looking around the room for Amelia. She comes skipping out of the guest bedroom, but to my dismay she's no longer wearing just my shirt and her white panties. She's changed into ripped jeans and a tight low-cut pink top, which is equally sexy on her, but nowhere near as sexy as the almost nothing she was wearing before.

"Ready to eat?" she asks, plopping into the chair next to me.

"Yes, everything looks great."

She smiles triumphantly and watches as I start dishing up my plate.

V. Kelly

"So, what did you want to talk to me about?" she asks, when we both have a good helping of food in front of us.

For a few wonderful moments I almost forgot about the impending doom looming on the horizon for her. There's no use waiting until the timing is right. I should rip the band-aid off now and prepare her for what's coming.

"Amelia, the insurance company called me today."

She side-eyes me as she stuffs her mouth with some spaghetti and briefly chews for a few seconds before asking, "What did they say?"

"They are looking to get out of paying you an insurance claim."

"Can they do that?"

I hesitate for a second and shovel a few bites of salad into my mouth. She gazes at me attentively until I swallow and take a drink of the wine she poured for me.

"Unfortunately, yes. I'm not going to lie to you; it doesn't look good. They want to prosecute you for arson."

"Arson?" she screeches. "Can they do that? I made a mistake. I never meant to set my house on fire. Did you tell them that?" I can already see tiny tears shimmering across her eyes.

"Yes, I did try to explain that to them. The problem is that you set fire to someone else's property and that fire is what caused your house to burn down. Arson is a felony and the State is looking to prosecute you."

"I can't go to jail, Ryker. Not for setting a bra on fire and some stupid expensive briefcase." She starts to hyperventilate so I take her hand.

"Look, Amelia. It's important that you stay calm right now. I know that everything around you seems to be imploding, but you can't freak out. I'm doing my best to keep you from going to prison, but what you did is technically arson. According to the law, if you damage someone's property with fire or explosives without their consent, or if you damage your personal property with the intent to defraud an insurance company, that's considered arson. At first, the insurance company believed that you set fire to your house with the intent on collecting the insurance money. I talked them out of that. But, because you set fire to Willis' belongings without his consent, they want to charge you with arson. If he presses charges against you, you could end up in jail."

I grip her hand when she begins lightly sobbing, hoping it will ease some of her pain. I know this has to be hard for her to hear, but she made a mistake, and now she's going to have to live with those consequences.

"I'm going to jail, aren't I?"

"No. Not if I have anything to say about it. If anything, you might end up with probation, but that's only if Willis doesn't press charges. The State might still want to prosecute you even if he decides not file a suit."

"Do you think Willis will press charges against me?"

"If he knows what's good for him, he won't. That boy fucked up and he deserved to get a few of his belongings burned. My aggression toward him in the hospital probably didn't help the situation, but I couldn't stand by and watch that little pissant grovel at your feet and beg for forgiveness. He doesn't deserve someone as amazing as you."

She looks up at me with her tear-filled blue eyes and smiles.

"You think I'm amazing?" she whispers.

I grab both of her hands and look into her eyes a little too intimately. "Of course! Amelia, besides Haysleigh, you're one of the most important people in my life. There's no woman in this world that can hold a candle to your beauty, and I'm not just saying that because you're like a daughter to me. I mean it."

She blinks slowly a few times like she's deciding what to say next. I never found blinking to be sexy before, but the way she's doing it right now is extremely attractive. I think it's her thick sultry lashes. Nothing is sexier than a woman with lashes that look like they can sweep a floor.

She squeezes my hands and links her fingers into mine. I swear I can feel her pulse racing through the webs of her fingers or maybe that's just my heart accelerating because the way she's touching me has a direct connection to my dick. Damn, she really needs to stop looking at me this way.

"I'm glad I'm not really your daughter," she whispers. It's barely audible, and if I wasn't good at lip reading, I would've never heard what she said.

"What was that?" I ask for clarification.

"Nothing. I'm just glad you're here for me. That's all."

She tries to cover up what she said, but I heard her very clearly. Internally, I'm glad that she's not biologically my daughter. It would be really inappropriate if she was my daughter and I was continuously undressing her with my eyes. On the flip side, it's probably best if I stopped feeling this way about her. Given her current situation with Haysleigh, it's best if I keep my distance, at least that way no one will get hurt. Especially, Haysleigh.

Amelia

I try to absorb everything Ryker told me over dinner, but my mind is imploding. In the hospital I was visited by a woman from the insurance company and I was under the impression that everything would be okay. She even helped me fill out my claim form. Now Ryker is telling me that there is a good chance my claim won't even go through and I might go to jail! How did I let this happen? Is my thirst for revenge outweighing my ability to form coherent thoughts and make good decisions?

Why did I set that fire? I've lost everything I love, and for what? Revenge. Ugh, revenge is supposed to be sweet, not one big fuck up that destroys everything you love.

Suddenly, my mind wanders to an image of my cat sitting next to me on the couch, his sleek gray fur is a silky smoothness that calms me down and creates a sense of peace inside of me.

I swallow hard.

Slinky! How have I not gone out looking for him yet?

I jump up from the bed in the guest bedroom and quickly throw on a light jacket and some comfortable shoes. It's dark outside—almost midnight. I have this overwhelming feeling that my cat is scared and out there somewhere in danger.

He needs me. I can feel it.

I carefully creep out into the hallway and pause when I reach Ryker's door. He's sound asleep because I can hear his adorable light snores filter into the hallway. As I pass by his door, a floorboard makes a hellacious creaking sound underneath my foot. It's so loud that it almost wakes up Ryker. I see him stir on his bed, the frame squeaking as he turns over and pulls the blanket over him more.

I could've asked him to come with me, but he's already done so much for me. This is something I need to do on my own. Slinky is my responsibility and I've already left him alone for far too long. My only hope is that he's stuck around my house—what's left of my house, that is.

I shut the front door and make sure that it makes as little sound as possible. The last thing I want to do is disturb Ryker when he's been working all day and has to go back in the morning.

My car still has a slight scent of smoke inside of it. It's a smell that I've tried to mask since I've gotten home, but it's like my car is filled with as much secondhand smoke as I am. I even attempted using five air fresheners to cover up the scent, but nothing works, not even the pungent woodsy smell from the fake little pine tree hanging from my rear-view mirror.

As I start my car it sputters, sounding too much like a cough. At least it's still running—at least there's that.

It takes me ten minutes to cross town. Once I turn on my old block PTSD hits me like a tidal wave. I see the fire again, blowing up in my face as it engulfs my house in angry flames. Tears immediately prick my eyes, especially when I pull into my old driveway.

My house is nothing but ash and burned wood now. It's even worse than when I came here with Ryker a few days ago. When I was here before, the frame was still slightly standing, but now everything is on the ground—a pile of rubbish nobody cares about except me.

I hesitate exiting the car. Anxiety swarms me like I'm sitting in a hive of bees. Flashbacks of the fire come at me like shrapnel.

I feel the anger inside of me again—building, growing, turning into the giant inferno swirling with revenge that made me squeeze the trigger of that fire lighter. Terror consumes my body. I feel the blast of the explosion hitting my face, the fear that raced through my bones when I saw my house go up in flames. I remember the panic that devoured me when I realized my cat was locked inside and I couldn't get to him, and the desperation I felt when my body couldn't move another inch, and the fire was licking my heels. The nightmares of that night fly at me, each piece of that memory slicing through my mind with the sharpness of broken glass. The tears are back, sliding down my face like lazy water slides as I remember what it was like to watch my grandparent's home go up in flames, and the guilt I felt knowing that I was the one who caused it.

I shake my head and try to steady my breath. There's a war going on inside of me and if I can't handle my emotions right now, I'll never find my cat.

"You can do this, Mia. Slinky needs you."

My hand fits around the handle, it's trembling as I push the door open.

What if my cat is dead?

That thought is even worse than the memories of the fire. If I lose Slinky, I lose everything I love. Without Haysleigh in my life, Slinky is the last piece of my past that I can hold on to that makes any sense.

Please don't be dead.

I exit my vehicle and slam the door shut. It's pitch-black outside. The streetlight near my former house has this bad habit

V. Kelly

of being out constantly. Damn, neighborhood kids like to throw rocks at it.

"Here, Kitty, Kitty," I yell, making a ticking sound with my mouth to call him.

The street is silent.

"Slinky cat, pretty, pretty cat. Come to Momma."

Nothing.

I start walking away from the car and over to the charred skeleton of my house.

"Kitty, Kitty, where are you?"

I start searching through the piles of rubble for any sign of my cat. He's probably long gone—or dead.

Why does that thought keep popping into my head?

I gotta face the facts, it's been five days. If he survived, he definitely wouldn't have stuck around.

I make my way out to the back alley and continue my search, using only the light of my phone to guide me. The back alley is thick with mud, it sticks to the bottom of my shoes as I search through piles of garbage, hoping by some slim chance Slinky will appear.

"Amelia?" a voice calls out from behind me.

I whip around and see Ryker standing behind the police tape.

"Ryker? What are you doing here?"

"I heard you leave. I was worried about you," he remarks, his eyes softening when he notices my furrowed brow.

"I'm just looking for Slinky."

Ryker walks through the debris and makes his way over to me. "Looking for your cat at midnight isn't the best idea, Amelia, especially not alone."

My head careens so I can look into his beautiful tawny colored eyes. They're hard to see in this light, but they briefly reflect in the light of my phone when I accidentally shine it at his face.

"I'm not alone now."

He smiles as he takes my hand. "You'll never be alone as long as I'm here."

I try to hide the nervous blush that creeps across my cheeks, but it's warming my face, along with the coy smile flirting with my lips.

"This is like looking for a needle in a haystack, isn't it?"

He nods. "Unfortunately."

"Should I give up?"

"No, let's walk up and down the block at least once before we head back. We're here, we might as well look for him now.

Ryker and I continue searching the alley. We stay out there for almost thirty minutes. We look under porches, wade through trash bags, and even searched through an old desk, hoping Slinky was hiding inside. I decided it was time to give up the search after seeing two scraggily alley cats getting it on behind a trashcan, and one questionable rat cut in front of me with a dead mouse in his snout.

"Nope, that's it, I'm done. This search is over for the night. I don't pal around with cannibal rats."

Ryker chuckles. "It wasn't the two cats mating that put you off?"

"Procreation is necessary for any species to survive. Though I'm not too keen on the cat's blatant voyeurism. That rat is basically a vermin serial killer creating mass genocide within his species. There's a huge difference."

Ryker's smile widens. "Yes, there is."

We make our way back to my car with my heart even more disheartened than before. Despair takes over me as we settle in front of my driver's side door. "I hope Slinky is okay. I hate thinking about him out here all alone. What if those skeezy alley cats coerce him into a threesome or something?"

"He'll be fine."

"How do you know?"

"Cats are resourceful. They're pretty good at protecting themselves. Slinky's not going to join in a threesome unless he wants to."

"I wish we had found him. You were right, it was a bad idea looking for him at night," I frown.

"Even though cats are nocturnal, the likelihood of Slinky hanging around your house after the traumatic event that unfolded the last time he was here, is not good. Looking for him during the day would be better. We could cover more ground that way."

I let out an exasperated breath. "I just miss him, Ryker. He's all I have left."

Ryker lightly cups my chin. "No, he's not, Amelia; you have me, too."

I nibble my lip, fighting the urge to kiss him. In a perfect world I could kiss him without regret or a hidden agenda, but with thoughts of revenge still floating around in my brain, I briefly wonder what would happen if I did kiss him and Haysleigh found out about it?

The thought makes me challenge the distance between us. I push myself against his body, admiring his rock-hard chest and soft cotton shirt. My hand grips onto the fabric and I pull him even closer to me, making his lips only inches away from my own.

Desire floods his eyes, before apprehension replaces it.

"Amelia?" he whispers.

"Yeah?" I murmur, inching even closer. My eyes flutter as they close, my body goading him to kiss me.

"We shouldn't do this."

"Why?"

"Because I don't think I can stop myself if I do." He pulls away. "And . . . I . . . just can't."

I chew on my next words very carefully. "Is it because of Haysleigh?"

He sighs, "Yes . . . and no."

My mouth ticks ever so slightly, and for some odd reason his rejection ignites a sudden need to cry.

"Hey, now. What's with the tears?" His rough thumb swipes away a few stray tears that have fallen over my cheek, while his other hand lightly plays with the tips of my messy blonde hair.

"I don't know," I answer honestly. "I feel like an idiot. I thought that maybe you liked me . . . you know like *liked* me. Now, I feel stupid for even making a slight advance towards you."

"Amelia . . ."

"Stop, don't call me that."

His hand is as big as my face, but the coarse texture of his palm is rather soothing against my cheek.

"Amelia, I know you're hurting right now, but I'm not the kind of man who will settle for being someone's rebound. You're not over Willis yet, and once you are, I'm sure you'll find someone perfect for you."

I found him when I was fifteen.

"Listen, Amelia, you're too emotional, and you're not thinking straight. These feelings you're feeling aren't real. They can't be."

They can.

V. Kelly

"One of these days a man is going to come into your life and sweep you off of your feet."

Already happened.

I gaze up at him, my bottom lip quivering with reckless need. Being this close to Ryker has my entire body trembling with desire. Revenge is still in the back of my mind, but right now, all I can think about is Ryker grabbing me by the shoulders, pulling me into his body, and pressing those full lips to mine so I can devour them.

"Stop looking at me like that."

"Like what?"

"Like you want me to kiss you."

I take a step back, removing myself from his embrace.

"Does this help?"

"No," he grumbles, his words catching in his throat. "We should go." He twitches nervously, moving his stance from one foot to the other.

"We should," I agree.

He's gonna kiss me.

"It's getting late."

"It really is," I murmur.

"It's after midnight," he reminds me.

"Cinderella would be jealous."

The corners of his lips lift upward, and I see the tension leave his shoulders. "Ah, hell. Fuck it!" he roars, before his hands grab my shoulders and pull me into him. His lips are next, claiming mine with a forceful possession that I can feel deep in my toes.

Haysleigh's dad is finally kissing me!

The man of my dreams—the man I've wanted since I was fifteen years old, is finally kissing me.

His fingers thread even deeper into my hair, slightly tugging on the roots as he commands our kiss. My hands wander up his biceps squeezing and feeling every inch I can while I have the opportunity to do it.

"More," I whisper into his lips.

His right hand wanders down my back side, gripping my ass firmly as he pushes my lower half into his. He's hard—every fucking amazing inch of him.

I moan ever so slightly and rock into him, making sure he knows how serious I am about this.

He suddenly pulls away, staring at me like he just made the biggest mistake of his life.

"I'm sorry, Mia!"

He called me Mia . . . My heart breaks a little.

"Ryker, it's okay. I wanted you to kiss me."

"No, none of this is okay. I overstepped a boundary in our relationship I should've never crossed. I'm so sorry. This . . . us . . . it will never happen again."

"Ryker."

He doesn't say another word to me as he flees to his car, leaving nothing but the ghost of his kiss behind him.

Ryker

"Brent, I need a fucking drink. Something hard that will make me forget the ten piles of dog shit I stepped in yesterday."

Brent, my friend and owner of B's Sports Bar, walks over to where I'm standing and starts pouring a shot of his best whiskey.

"Want to talk about it?" He slides the glass across the bar and into my awaiting hands. "On the house," he exclaims watching as I take down the fiery whiskey in one gulp.

"Blech, I forgot how much I hate hard liquor."

Brent chuckles, "You asked for something hard."

"And you produced it. I grew eight chest hairs downing that shit." I wipe my mouth and toy with the glass, before signaling for one more shot.

Brent fills my shot glass and leans over the bar. The place is dead, which is why I love Thursday nights. Brent gives us a deal where we get two pints of his best beer for eight dollars. Sometimes, Thursdays are busy, but tonight it's a ghost town.

"So, Ryker, what happened that's got you filling up on the hard stuff?"

I let out a long, exasperated sigh. "Ever want a woman so bad, but you know there's no way you can have her?"

"Every time a beautiful girl walks into this bar," he chuckles.

"Well, I did something yesterday that I regret. I kissed my daughter's best friend. They're kinda going through a rough patch right now, but she's been my daughter's friend for as long as I can remember. She's staying with me for a while until she can get back on her feet. I thought I could keep my hands to myself, but then she looked up at me with those typical *fuck me eyes* and my dick decided to start thinking for me."

Brent studies my expression, obviously noticing the way my brow is narrowed with both sexual frustration and self-loathing. Our kiss has been on my mind since it happened. I can still feel her lips, soft like newly fallen snow, and reckless like a teenager on a joy ride. I grip the glass even tighter, remembering the perfection of her tongue invading my mouth and teasing the tops of my lips.

I have to adjust because, yeah, thinking about that kiss has me fucking hard again.

"Seems to me, you have a problem, my friend."

"Yeah, I have a twenty-one-year-old, hot-as-fuck problem."

He whistles, before an envious grin spreads across his face. "Twenty-one, huh?"

"Totally legal. Totally off-limits," I grumble, downing my shot in one gulp. The burn isn't as bad this time, but my taste buds are cursing me for subjecting them to the Devil's brew again.

"Why does she have to be off-limits?"

I give him a pained look. "She's almost sixteen years younger than me, Brent, and my daughter's best friend. Well, ex-best friend."

Brent takes the shot glass from my hand and places it underneath the bar. "Let me tell you something, Ryker. Life is too short to be hung up on age and technicalities. Do you like the girl?"

"Yes. I may even love her," I admit. Though saying those words out loud when our relationship is still strictly platonic is like having a prisoner stab a shiv into my kidney. There's no way a relationship would ever work between us. Not if Haysleigh has anything to say about it.

"Then why put your feelings aside? I know she's your daughter's friend, but you've been out of the game for so long. You deserve to follow your heart, Ryker, even if that heart belongs to your daughter's best friend."

I nod, my eyes slightly crossing when the whiskey starts to mess with my thoughts. This is why I don't drink whiskey.

"Your cousin is here," Brent tells me, motioning to the door.

I look over my shoulder and notice Chase heading over to our normal table. By the time I look back, Brent has already placed two pitchers of beer on the bar. The man is magical.

"Ask Chase his opinion," Brent laughs, "we both know he's been in your shoes before."

"Thanks, Brent," I say, as I slide him a twenty-dollar bill, not even caring about my change. I turn and walk toward our usual table with the pitchers in hand.

"Hey, Ryker," Chase greets me. He pulls out a chair before he plops down into it.

I place the two pitchers of beer on the table and sit across from him.

"Hey, Chase, how's life?" I study my cousin for a few minutes, wondering how I should bring up my little Amelia problem. His history with dating younger women is bad, and I don't want to unearth old demons that he's tried so hard to bury.

About a year ago, Chase got involved with one of his students. It turned out to be one of the worst mistakes he ever made. Their relationship was a tumultuous love affair, one that cost him his job, his house, and his relationship with his son. He spent the last twelve months trying to find himself. I had to pick up the pieces a few times. There were days I would find him passed out on his floor or drinking his sorrows away. He says he didn't love the girl, but you don't go through that much grief and self-loathing after a break-up without some sort of love hidden behind it. He seems to be doing better, but I can see that the relationship still haunts him.

"Today's been the fucking day from hell," he remarks as he rubs a frustrated hand over his beard.

I stare at his beard with envy. I've always tried to grow a beard, but I was blessed with a baby's face. I can grow stubble and rock a nice five o'clock shadow any day of the week, but when I actually try to grow out my facial hair, it looked like I stuck pubes all over my face. Chase could shave his face and wake up the next day still looking like a lumberjack.

"How so?"

"I had five job interviews today, but no bites. I can't keep slinging burgers for the rest of my life. That little studio apartment I have is starting to feel really crowded."

I can see the pain in his eyes. He went from having one of those nice houses with a picket fence, to nothing in the matter of months. Once he lost his job, he couldn't afford that nice house anymore. His ex-wife Bethany found out about his little affair and ran off with their son to Florida. Since then, he's been doing whatever he can to regain partial custody. I feel bad for my cousin. I spent most of our teenage years trying to mold him into the man he is now, but one little love affair with a young, hot piece of ass wrecked everything for him. I tried to talk him out of it, but he wouldn't listen.

"I miss teaching," he informs me, grabbing one of the glasses off the table that Brent brought over while we were talking. "Thanks, Brent." He salutes him with his beer and recklessly starts chugging it.

V. Kelly

"Do you think drinking like that is a good idea?" I question when the beer starts spilling down his face and catches in his beard. I worry he's going to fall off the wagon again. The last time he drank this carelessly, I had to take him to the hospital.

"Nope. It's an awful idea, but it helps numb the squirrels fucking in my head right now."

"How about I try to take your mind off your troubles? I have a problem, one that I think you can help me with."

Chase looks intrigued and sits up in his chair. I'm about to tell him all about what happened with Amelia, but we're interrupted by our other drinking buddies, Finn and Scott, who suddenly appear at the table.

"What's up fuckers," Scott yells, "You can all rejoice because the king has finally arrived!"

I'm not Scott's biggest fan. He's a pompous asshole with a rich boy complex. He's brash and vulgar. He throws money around like it's nothing, and I hate that he uses women like they're toilet paper—they're okay to wash his dick with but only good for one flush. His cavalier attitude with the ladies is repulsive at best. He even talked himself into a threesome with Chase and his student. How he did that, I have no idea. There's no way I'd let Scott within three feet of Haysleigh or Amelia.

Even though I think Scott's a prick ninety-five percent of the time, being friends with someone whose pockets are lined with hundred-dollar bills does come in handy at times. He helped me out of a jam when I couldn't afford to get groceries and needed to feed Haysleigh. He also helped Finn start up his app company. He's technically a silent partner, but Chase and I aren't supposed to know that. I guess it's true what they say . . . underneath all that asshole is actually a heart of gold. But like the elusive pot-of-gold you find at the end of a rainbow, Scott's golden heart only appears when the conditions are just right.

I'm not sure why Finn hangs out with him so much. He's Scott's opposite. He's always been the quiet, shy guy who cowers behind a nerdy exterior. For a guy, he's actually not bad looking. I think it's hilarious that he's still a virgin, because if the guy tried a little harder, he'd have pussy flung at him with a sling shot.

"So, what's troubling ya, Ryker?" Scott asks, slapping me on the back.

I don't really want to talk about Amelia in front of Scott. He's always been the most vocal about changing the platonic status of my relationship with Amelia to something sexual. If he had his way, I would've fucked her when she was fifteen when we all noticed how nice her tits were starting to look in low-cut tops. His major playboy attitude is something I despise. I hate the way he looks at Haysleigh; he stares at her like she's a lamb, and he wants to hit her with his big bad wolf. Yeah, not fucking happening.

"Amelia is going to be staying with me for a while. Her house caught on fire after she burned all of her boyfriend's shit in the backyard. This was after she caught him fucking Haysleigh in their bedroom."

"Holy fuck!" Scott shouts. "That's some straight up *Jerry Springer* shit right there. I don't see how that's a problem. You got a fucking hot piece of ass at your disposal. Spread the bitch's legs and stick your old man in that young twat. Young pussy is good for the soul." He grins, so I know he's kidding, but I'm on the verge of throwing him across the bar and kicking the shit out of him.

V. Kelly

"Watch your fucking mouth, Scott, before I fucking throw you into that jukebox."

"Hey now, you know I'm fucking with you, Ryker. We all know how you feel about Amelia. That bitch's pussy had you whipped the second it sprouted pubes."

I grip my beer, ready to shower him with the contents before smashing the stein over his smug face. I could do it. It would be fun as hell, but I know the bastard can't help the filth that flaps from his gums. He's a narcist and reacting to his bullshit will only inflate his repulsive ego.

Chase and Finn look between us, knowing damn well that if Scott doesn't shut up, I won't be able to control my anger any longer.

"What exactly is your problem, Ryke?" Chase asks, diverting the attention away from Scott.

"I kissed Amelia last night. I kissed the girl and I liked it." I should be smiling, but the guilt eats my insides like a hungry caterpillar.

"No, you loved it!" Scott yells louder. "You were like. Oh, yeah! Right there, baby. Then you pounded that fine ass pussy like a damn jackhammer." Scott stands up and does this obnoxious jerking motion with his pelvis, making what sounds like machine gun sounds with his mouth.

"I hate you sometimes, Scott," I growl.

"Tell me you fucked her." He grabs my shirt and starts shaking me. "I've been wanting to hit that pussy since the first time I laid eyes on her. Tell me you hit that snatch like a fucking boxer. POW BAM! POW BAM!"

Sometimes I wonder if Scott has ADHD, his hyperactivity is extremely off-putting.

I look over at Chase who is shaking his head while trying to hold in his laughter.

"What do you think I should do, Chase?"

He shrugs his shoulders. "Don't look at me, Ryke. You know how I feel about dating younger women. My experience fucked up my life."

"That's because you got feelings involved. What you need to do, Ryker, is go home, fuck that bitch's pussy and come all up in that shit until you fill her with all your baby juice. Claim that shit and make it yours, Ryke. Knock that bitch up. We all know how you feel about her. It's about time you get some action that doesn't involve your hand."

I grab Scott's shirt and pull him toward me.

"Call her a bitch one more time. I dare you."

Finn interjects to break the tension, "Ryker, I think what Scott's trying to say is that you've loved this girl for a very long time. Even if you don't want to admit it, it's true. We all see it. This isn't like Chase's situation. You've got a history with this girl—sixteen years of it. If you guys kissed, then that must mean she's feeling the same way about you. Why not explore what happens? What can it hurt?"

"My daughter, who just so happens to not be friends with her at the moment."

"That's cause she's a horny little slu . . ." Scott stops his next words when he sees my hands ball up into fists. "I'm just going to stop talking."

"Probably the best idea you've ever had, Scott," Chase grins, before looking over at me. "I'm with the boys. You know how I feel about age gaps, but I also know how you feel about Amelia. My suggestion is to see what happens. If it doesn't work out, it doesn't work out."

V. Kelly

"Maybe you guys are right."

"We are," Scott laughs, "I'm always right about pussy. Speaking of which, have you fucked that cute little intern yet, Finn?"

An embarrassed blush invades Finn's face. It crawls down his neck and his nose turns slightly red like he's Rudolph.

"No. She's just an intern."

"An intern that's all over his junk," Scott exclaims looking around the table. "I went to visit his sorry ass last week. You know, to see how things were going with his new app. So, we're in the room talking and all of a sudden, this sexy little blonde chick comes sashaying into his office in a low-cut top, fucking pencil skirt, and fishnet tights. I gave her the once over, even fluffed myself up like a peacock to get her attention and this chick didn't even look at me as she walks over to Finn's desk."

Scott's talking animatedly with his hands, waving them around like he's invoking his inner mime. It's comical to watch, but poor Finn looks absolutely mortified that he's telling us the story.

"As she places his coffee in front of him, she dangles her big old titties in his face. At first, Finny here didn't notice, but then he looks up and I swear to God, this mother fucker popped a tent so fast that it broke a button. I shit you not. That fucking button went flying off his pants and hit the wall. Fucking funniest shit, I've ever seen in my life. You'd think the girl would've run for the hills, but then she grabs a safety pin off the side of her skirt, and drops to her fucking knees, pinning that shit up for our dear friend Finn. She didn't even ask for permission. She just squatted, grabbed his pants, and pinned that shit together. Finn was so red I thought he was going to hyperventilate. Then, as if all this shit wasn't enough, his little intern tells him that if he needs anything, emphasis on anything, she was just a phone call away. That bitch wants to take Finn's virginity for a spin." I think Scott barely breathed while retelling his story.

I have to admit; the whole situation does sound kind of hot.

"She doesn't like me. She was just being nice," Finn blushes.

"Did she touch your cock?" I ask.

"Briefly," he admits.

"Then she wants to fuck you, Finn. You're thirty years old and a goddamn virgin, I think it's time that you cash in that V-card and bend that little intern over your desk. She needs a good spanking." Scott waggles his eyebrows at Finn.

All this sex talk is helping me with my Amelia situation. I wonder what she's doing right now?

"Stop it, Scott, you're scaring the poor guy," Chase jokes.

"I'm not scared," Finn grumbles, "I'm just saving myself for marriage."

"Good little Christian boys need to be fucking spanked, too, Finn. Fuck all that bible-thumping, save yourself for marriage bullshit. Your cock is malnourished and hungry. Let it eat at the twat buffet for a little while before you put a ring on it."

Finn's cheeks redden even more. Scott's favorite pastime is making Finn feel uncomfortable.

Chase notices Finn's discomfort and changes the topic. He's really good at that. "Anyway, Ryker, my advice is to see what happens with Amelia. At least then, you won't be asking yourself what would've happened if you fucked your daughter's best friend."

In my slightly inebriated state, they were making total sense. Amelia and Haysleigh's relationship is on the rocks, and there's no reason I can't explore something with Amelia.

V. Kelly

Haysleigh will have to understand. She fucked Willis for revenge but fell in love with him, there's not much difference in me falling for her best friend. Is there?

"Maybe you're right. I'll go home and talk to her about it. We're both grown-ups, I'm sure we can come to a mutual consensus about the kiss and decide like adults what to do from there."

"That a boy," Scott congratulates me, slapping me on the back. "Go home and tear her pussy up."

I glare at him. "You're sick."

"Sick of being in a dry spell. If I don't get some quality punani quick, I may shrivel up and die. Maybe I need to find myself some super young pussy, too. Everyone else at this table seems to be doing it."

"You act like you weren't doing it first," I laugh. "You're the king of young pussy, Scott."

"Not true my friend. I've never slept with a girl *that* much younger than me before. Not that I haven't wanted to. One day I will, but I need to find the right girl who's worth the hassle. Young bitches get caught up in their feelings and shit."

"You're a piece of work," Finn exclaims. "Sometimes I wonder how we're still friends."

"Face it, Finny, I keep your life interesting. Without me you'd all be a bunch of boring old men drinking at an empty sports bar. You keep me around as comic relief."

"Preach," I say aloud, causing everyone at the table to look at me. I shrug off their unwanted stares. "What? We all know that there's only one thing Scott's good at, and that's running his big, fat mouth."

Finn and Chase nod their heads in agreement.

Scott chuckles and takes a sip of his beer. I see his lips slide mischievously behind the glass.

Oh no, here we go.

"The ladies love my mouth, boys. I tongue swab pussies like a fucking gynecologist. That's why you should listen to me, Ryker. Amelia is a hot piece of ass. Now that she's single, guys are gonna sniff out her pussy like it's a fucking all you can eat barbecue joint. The longer you hold off fucking her, the more likely someone else is going to swoop in and steal her out from under you. Do us all a favor. Hop in your truck, drive home, and fuck that little bit . . . I mean Amelia, before some tool decides to take her for a test run."

I grip my glass even tighter. I don't like the idea of any man touching Amelia.

"You know he's right, Ryker. If you don't move in and claim Amelia's pussy as your own, some other dick will," Chase agrees.

"All she needs is your mushroom head stamp of approval, Ryker," Scott jokes.

I look over at Finn. "What do you think?"

He shrugs. "Don't look at me. I'm the virgin at this table. My sexual experiences are limited to computer screens and personal hand jobs." He waves his fingers at me, "I'm my dick's only friend."

Chase and I smirk at each other, before we both start laughing. Finn's starting to sound more and more like Scott every day. It's good that he's finally breaking out of his nerdy bubble, but the last person he needs to idolize is someone like Scott.

Scott looks around the table like a proud papa. He wipes away a fake tear because he's an ass like that. "That's my Finny. Right now, he's tugging his ding-a-ling like a happy little tugboat.

V. Kelly

Tomorrow, he'll be popping pussy pills like the rest of us." Scott looks back over at me and grins. "Are you gonna claim that pussy or do I have to do it for you?"

I finally give in, because all of them are right. If I don't claim her, someone else will, and it sure as hell won't be fucking Scott.

"Alright, I'm gonna head out and talk to Amelia. After the way I left her last night, she deserves a one-on-one conversation."

Scott smiles evilly, "You mean a nice one-under-one conversation. P ... pa ... pound that shit for me," he stutters, disguising his voice like Porky Pig. He holds up his fist and I reluctantly fist bump it. I shouldn't encourage him, but Scott comes up with some funny as hell shit sometimes.

I throw a fist bump Finn and Chase's way, before leaving the table.

After the way I acted last night, the least I can do is talk to Amelia about what happened. I feel like an ass for leaving her like that, but if I didn't remove myself from the situation, I was going to do something I would've regretted. At least I have a better head about all of this. Now, all I have to do is tell her that it can't happen again.

Amelia

I'm in his bed again.

After the fiasco that happened last night, I had to work off some of this pent-up sexual frustration. I tried masturbating in my own bed, but it wasn't the same. I needed to picture him—to feel closer to him—to smell him. His sheets smell like a man: a mix of Axe body spray, smoke, and fresh linen. It's intoxicating and exhilarating. Like a drug I never knew I needed.

I didn't mean to end up in his bed again, but it was the only way to relieve the major case of lady blue balls he gave me last night. Yes, girls can get blue balls, too. Although, ours should be called something for fitting like vagina deprivation syndrome.

This time, I have no idea when Ryker will be back. Not that I care. I have to get myself off, otherwise my pussy is gonna turn purple and wilt away.

I decided to wear his shirt again. I've worn it almost every night since I got here. Something about sleeping in Ryker's shirt calms me down and makes me feel at peace.

I wish he was here right now. He could run those manly hands over the hills of my breasts and help fix the problem he left my pussy with last night.

Doing this again on Ryker's bed makes me feel reckless and devious. Like I'm the dirty little secret Ryker keeps hidden away.

"I'm such a naughty girl," I moan as my hand slides over my clit and begins rubbing it with soft circles. In my head, I'm picturing Ryker fucking me from behind. His massive hands grip my hips as he roughly pounds my pussy with his throbbing cock. I rub even harder, picturing how his cock would feel in between my folds. It's that thought that sends me over the edge.

"Fuck me, Ryker! Fuck me now!" I scream. I'm moaning so loudly that I don't hear footsteps racing down the hall until it's too late.

Just as I hit my climax, the door swings violently open. My head shoots up in surprise, but I'm so caught up in my orgasm that my fingers never leave my pussy. I stare Ryker dead in the eye while I finish myself off; my body spasming, adrenaline rushing like I'm running only on endorphins. I can't believe I'm doing this in front of him, but I don't want to stop. Not when his eyes are filled with a deadly lust that I'm desperate to capture.

His mouth slightly hangs open, as his eyes focus on what I'm doing between my legs. His eyes slowly rove over my body like he's drinking everything in and recording it to memory. I like the way he's looking at me. The nervous nibble of the corner of his lip, the slight smirk as my hand finally leaves my clit.

I don't know what to say, so I sit up on my elbows and look at him, challenging him with my eyes.

"Oh, hey," I murmur. Seduction is key here. He's already caught me masturbating on his bed, so there's no point in trying to hide it. Acting casual like there's nothing wrong with what's happening is the only way to go into this situation.

"Amelia, what are you doing?" he questions. He nervously undoes the top button of his shirt, tugging at the collar as if it's suddenly too tight.

Is that sweat dripping down his forehead?

Am I making him nervous?

"I'm pretty sure you know exactly what's going on," I smile deviously. It's time to challenge our relationship.

He looks visibly shaken but hasn't left the room. That's a good sign. He stares at the open shirt I'm wearing because it's barely covering my breasts and licks his lips. Then his eyes wander down my torso until they settle on my legs, which are still opened in a very provocative position.

Yup, I'm wearing no panties. My pussy is on full display.

I know I should cover myself up, but his predatory gaze has me wondering what's going to happen next.

"You're masturbating on my bed?" he shouts, his tone verging on angry.

"Yes." I can feel my cheeks start to flush with embarrassment. This is not the reaction I was hoping for.

What is he thinking?

Should I get up and put my clothes back on?

Did I make him angry?

"I'm sorry, I shouldn't have done this," I start to apologize. "This was a mistake."

An angry scowl takes over his brow.

Ugh, that look on his face says it all. This was definitely a mistake.

"I'm sorry. I'm so, so sorry." I don't like apologizing for something I'm not really sorry for, but I also don't want him to be angry with me.

"I don't know what to say."

At least he doesn't sound angry this time. He must notice how nervous and embarrassed I am.

I start to cover myself up and move to get off the bed, but he puts up a hand to stop me. "Please don't get up."

"Why?"

"Because as perverted as this sounds, what you just did was amazing. Walking in here to find you fingering yourself on my bed; damn, that was fucking hot. God, you're so beautiful, Amelia. Every damn inch of you is fucking perfect. So, please don't cover up. This may be the only time I get to see you this way. I don't want you to ruin the moment."

Did Haysleigh's dad just call me perfect?

He takes a cautious step into the room. As he does, my eyes skim down his muscular body, stopping at the tent party going on in his pants.

Oh my God! Ryker has a hard-on. He has a hard-on and it's because of me.

"You should cover yourself up before I do something, we both will regret." There's a strange frustration in his voice. I can see the tension set in his jaw. His hand quickly adjusts the "tent", because it's seconds away from *Hulk-smashing* through his zipper.

"I'm sorry, Ryker. I didn't mean to offend you."

"Oh, Amelia, you didn't offend me, quite the opposite really. Every inch of me is dying to be inside of you. I hope you don't take that the wrong way, but you're incredibly beautiful and it's impossible for any man to not want you." He covers his face with his arm and looks towards the door. "God, I'm such a pervert."

"You're not a pervert, Ryker," I blurt. "I'm the pervert for masturbating on your bed. I wish I could say this is my first time, but it's not. I've actually done this before. So, if anyone is perverted, it's me. I couldn't help myself. Your bed smells like you, and I'm sorry, but I've always had a sort of schoolgirl crush on you. Being alone in this house made me feel very vulnerable after what happened last night between us. I wasn't sure if you were reciprocating my feelings and everything made me horny— God, I've been so fucking horny since I got here. I couldn't shake my sexual frustrations, and I got a little carried away, but I promise it won't happen again."

Ryker uncovers his eyes and looks at me strangely. "You have a crush on me?"

I nod. "For as long as I can remember. I used to secretly wish that you'd be the one to take my virginity, but I knew that would never happen because you're Haysleigh's dad and I'm so much younger than you. You've always been so off limits, but now that Haysleigh and I aren't talking, I couldn't help getting caught up in the fantasy of what it would be like to be with you. I promise it won't happen again. This was a two-time masturbation incident."

His eyes meet mine, and like a tumultuous whirlpool, I can see the lust swirling inside of them.

"Amelia, I'm only going to say this once. That kiss last night was everything. I can't stop thinking about how soft your fucking lips are or how they made me feel. I'm sixteen years older than you, but I find you incredibly attractive. I've done my best to fight my attraction, but it's getting harder the older you get. It would be in our best interest if you get up off my bed and leave now, because I have about a thirty second window before I can't contain myself anymore. I'm seconds away from pushing you back down on that bed and fingering you myself, if you choose to stay here any longer. That means I won't be a gentleman, and this father/daughter relationship we have will be thrown out the fucking window."

His words strike every horny nerve in my body. I swear my pussy gets wetter with each possessive word.

Do I really want to pass up the opportunity to be touched by Ryker? Should I really cross this line we've put up between each other?

V. Kelly

Yes. Yes, I should.

I don't move.

"Amelia, I'm not kidding."

"Neither am I," I whisper, falling back onto his comforter. "I'm not going anywhere so you're either going to have to leave the room or fuck me. Your choice."

Ryker growls, releasing some of his sexual frustration. It's the most animalistic sound I've ever heard, and I find it incredibly sexy. He kicks off both his shoes, slams the door closed behind him, and locks it. Then I watch in utter fascination as he removes every article of clothing on his body, only stopping when he hits his briefs. They're a dark blue color and currently stretched out by his rock-hard cock.

"If we do this . . . there's no turning back," he states, falling onto the bed beside me.

I undo a button on my shirt and tease him by slowly undoing another.

Ryker licks his lips, his tan skin flushing a light shade of pink when he sees the first peek of my nipple appear.

I slowly start working on the last few buttons, but I must be going too slow for him, because Ryker grabs each side of the shirt and shreds the fabric in his big burly hands. Pearly white buttons go flying across the room, one smacks me in the forehead before rolling onto the floor. Another I hear hit the wall and then something metal on his dresser.

He stares at my naked body with approving eyes. First, he admires my pert nipples and then the neatly trimmed hair above my pussy. I cut it into a cute little racing stripe the morning before I found Willis in bed with Haysleigh. I was expecting Willis to be the one to appreciate my craftsmanship but having Ryker's wandering eyes perusing my artwork is so much better.

"Give me permission to touch you, Amelia. Tell me what I can do to you."

"Ryker, you can do whatever you want to me. All I want is to feel your hands on my body. Please don't make me wait any longer. I need this. I need you."

He shakes his head and smirks. "This must be a dream."

"This isn't a dream, Ryker. I want you to touch me. Shit, tease me while you're at it. Do whatever you want with me, but don't make me wait one second longer." I lie back, running my fingers over my nipples, making sure they're budded and ready.

Ryker's eyes close, almost as if he's talking himself out of touching me, but then he moves towards me. He grabs my ankle. In one possessive move he has me pinned underneath him, my breasts pressed into his chest, his hand gripping the flesh of my ass. His eyes penetrate me with a fierce intensity I can feel deep inside my core.

"Touch me, Ryker," I beg, bucking my hips so they rub against his hard cock. "Please."

He dips down to finish what we started last night. His kiss is gentle at first, then it turns more aggressive. He sucks my bottom lip into his mouth right before his tongue darts inside for a taste. For a few seconds our tongues silently dance together, hands roving over each other's exposed skin. It's the most seductive kiss I've ever experienced, and before I know what's happening, my hands are up in his hair, tearing at the roots as he kisses his way down my body.

He stops just above my nipple and frowns. "Do you think we should stop?"

"No!" I screech, pulling his hair even harder. "I think we should keep going."

V. Kelly

He smiles, then sucks my nipple between his lips. He makes a loud popping sound when he releases it, then follows it up with a few swift licks.

"How long have you wanted me to do this to you, Amelia?"

I meet his eyes. He smiles as he kisses and nips his way down my center until he's got his mouth hovering just above my pussy. He gently blows on it, igniting every endorphin inside of me.

"Ryker, I've been wanting to do this since I was fifteen years old. That's how obsessed with you I am."

My words are cut off by him pressing his lips to my clit and the hard suction that follows. I scream out, digging my fingers even harder into his scalp, and before I even have a chance to enjoy it, I'm already coming all over his gorgeously tan face.

Damn, that was fast.

Ryker

Amelia squeezes my head with her thighs. Her entire body rocks and bucks against my face as she he's hit with an intense orgasm.

Did she really just say she's wanted me since she was fifteen?

The thought of Amelia reciprocating my feelings makes me a little apprehensive. I shouldn't be doing this. I should be politely turning her down, but my attraction and feelings for her overrule my conscience, and I work even harder to get her to her second orgasm. This time I hook my finger inside of her pussy while I tease her clit with my tongue. I know from experience that pleasing a woman from both sides is one of the quickest ways to get her to climax. She writhes erotically on the bed, before pushing me away with her hand because she can't take the sensation anymore.

"Stop," she breathes. Her voice cracks a bit, and for a second, I feel like I've fucked up somehow.

Now that I've tasted her, I need more. There's no turning back, but will she let me do anything else to her?

"It's my turn now," she says seductively. She pushes me aggressively on the bed and shimmies out of my shirt before pulling my briefs off and throwing them across the room.

She kisses the V that leads down to my dick, making sure to brush her soft cheek against my incredibly hard cock as she moves down my body. Then, without warning, her hot mouth engulfs it, sucking me in until my tip tickles her tonsils.

V. Kelly

Damn, does she even have a gag reflex?

She moves up and down my shaft, changing the way she uses her mouth every few strokes.

"You're bigger than I remember," she giggles. Stroking my cock slowly before swabbing it with her tongue.

"You were fifteen when you saw my dick, shouldn't it look smaller?" I joke.

She winks at me. "No, it's definitely bigger."

She sucks the tip of my dick hard, her cheeks indenting as the suction is focused solely on my erection. She lightly cups my balls, giving them a teasing squeeze before she flicks my tip playfully with her tongue.

Damn, she's sexy.

I think she knows she has me on the verge of exploding, because she stops when she sees my body start tense.

"Can I feel what it's like to have you inside me?" She crawls up my body, taking my shaft along her slit when she's at the right angle.

She doesn't even need to ask. I help her hand guide me toward her entrance and then slowly enter, pushing myself deeper and deeper until I'm buried inside.

Fuck. She feels even better than I imagined.

She starts moving her body on top of me, slow at first, then faster when she hears me grunt and groan with approval.

"Damn, you feel amazing."

"I want you to fuck me, Ryker. I want you to do it hard and fast. I remember hearing you in here fucking other women when I was younger. It made me so jealous. I know you can make a woman scream. So, make me scream, Ryker. Possess me the way you did them."

I grab her hips and shift so I'm on top of her. She stares up at me with those enormous sky-blue eyes, begging me to make her mine. What she doesn't know is that all those women that came before her meant nothing to me. Nobody will ever mean as much to me as Amelia does. Nobody.

I thrust into her hard and fast. Her head bounces off the bed, her entire body careening to fit against me. It's been a long time since a woman has been able to move her hips in tandem with each of my thrusts. Perks of fucking someone young that has flexibility, I guess. I bend in to kiss her—something I haven't done while fucking a woman in a long time.

Her fingers dig into the flesh of my back and she screams against my mouth. The clench of her pussy around my cock lets me know that she's orgasming again.

The grip her pussy has on my cock is too much, and I come so hard and so fast inside of her, that I'm immediately hit with a wave of dizziness.

"Damn," I manage to get out, collapsing on top of her. "That was amazing."

When I look down, Amelia is crying, and my heart shatters apart.

"Baby, what's wrong?"

She doesn't say anything. Instead, she pulls herself into a fetal position, and cowers against me, weeping into my chest.

"Amelia, what's going on?"

She looks up at me with little tears streaking down her beautiful cheeks. I wipe them away, bending down to kiss her pouting lips.

"Please tell me what's wrong."

Her eyes dart to the left, then the right, refusing to look me in the eye.

V. Kelly

"Amelia, talk to me. We shared this beautiful, intimate moment together, and now you have me second guessing if it was a mistake."

Her bottom lip quivers. "It wasn't a mistake. It was perfect— you . . . you are perfect." She cups my cheek and I nuzzle her palm. Her touch feels wonderful.

"I don't deserve someone like you. You saved my life and let me stay in your home, even though your daughter and I hate each other. I don't want to come between you and Haysleigh. I may hate the girl right now, but I don't want this—whatever this is, to affect your bond with her."

"It won't. Haysleigh is a big girl. She'll understand once I decide to tell her."

"Tell her what? How are you going to tell her that you fucked her ex-best friend without her getting upset?"

"No, I didn't fuck her best friend, I fell in love with her best friend." I take a strand of her hair, it's wet and sticking to the sweat on her face and move it behind her ear. "I know this sounds crazy, but I think I'm in love with you, Amelia. I think I've been in love with you for a very long time. I've kept my feelings hidden for all these years because I thought that you would never feel the same way, and that I was some old pervert fantasizing about my daughter's best friend. After our kiss last night, I was planning on coming home to tell you that we needed to take things slowly with one another, but I was open to exploring whatever is going on between us. Then I walked in and saw you naked on my bed with your fingers deep inside that sweet pussy. There was no taking it slow anymore. I wanted to be inside of you, claim you, force you to realize that we're meant to be together. You always have my emotions pacing inside of me like a captive tiger. I need to be with you, Amelia. I can't hold back my feelings any longer. Haysleigh will have to understand and accept us. She has to."

Her head slightly nods, but she still buries her face into my chest. "Ryker, I have major feelings for you, too, but I really should tell you something before we go any further. I . . ."

I cut her off, running my palm down the side of her wet cheeks, swiping away the stray tears messing up her beautiful complexion. I don't want her to cry, not after we shared something so beautiful. "We can talk later. Right now, I just want to fall asleep with you in my arms. It's something I've dreamt about doing for as long as I can remember."

There's nothing I want more than for her to tell me all her thoughts and feelings, but right now, I want to enjoy holding her in my arms and waking up beside her in the morning. It's the perfect way to end this perfect dream we are sharing.

I turn her body so I can spoon her. She settles in, fitting inside every crevice of my body like she's modeling clay modeled perfectly for me. She snuggles into me, but I can feel her body trembling as she silently sobs. I want to ask her what's wrong, but I also don't want to ruin the moment.

I'll talk to her in the morning, then we can sort out what to do next about us. There's no turning back now that we've had sex. I'm going to have to figure out a way to talk to Haysleigh about this. Hopefully she will understand—I have to make her understand.

Amelia

I wake up tangled in a web of muscles and bare chest. Everything felt like a dream last night, but here I am, sleeping in Ryker's bed . . . naked. I pinch my arm to see if I'm still dreaming, but I'm not.

I'm afraid to wake him as I unwind his arms from around my torso. He's sound asleep, so he doesn't do anything but moan in protest and turn over.

I carefully tiptoe to the guest bedroom and grab some clothes to change into, before walking to the bathroom to take a shower. The water feels amazing against my skin, warming it like Ryker's hands did last night. I take a little longer than usual to shower.

Thoughts of last night flood my brain, and regret overwhelms me once again. After we had sex, I started bawling. Guilt is such an overwhelming emotion. Everything I hoped for is finally happening . . . I made Ryker fall for me; I ended up in his bed; I have the perfect fuel to fuck up Haysleigh's world . . . only, I don't want revenge anymore. I want Ryker. I want to spend the rest of my life in his bed, waking up in those protective arms, kissing that smiling face. I want it all, knowing damn well that what I want can't happen. The second Haysleigh finds out about us, it's over. Ryker will be forced to choose between us. He'll have to choose her. Tears start falling from my eyes, mixing with the water tumbling out of the faucet above my head. How am I supposed to go to work this morning? If I leave, all of this will be over.

"Amelia? Are you okay?" I see Ryker's strong body through the fogged-up glass. He's still naked and as handsome as I remember.

"Yes . . ." I lie, hoping he'll leave.

He doesn't.

Ryker opens the shower door and walks inside, his masculine body taking up most of the space in the tiny stall. He smiles down at me, his cheeks slightly lifting into not fully formed dimples. He stretches out his forearm, lightly grasping my wrist so he can pull me into him.

I rush into his arms, holding as tight as I can, because it feels like this will be our last time holding each other like this.

"Amelia? What's wrong?"

I force myself to look into his eyes, not able to hide my tears behind the water anymore.

"I'm being emotional," I admit. "I feel like what happened last night was a onetime thing, and we can't be together."

"Why do you feel that way?"

"Haysleigh," I breathe.

He nods in agreement. "I'm still trying to figure out what I need to say to her. I shouldn't feel this way about you, Amelia. I'm sixteen years older than you."

"I know."

"This doesn't make any sense."

In my heart, it makes perfect sense.

"I shouldn't love you." His words pierce my soul and dismantle it. "But I do."

He cups my chin, forcing me to look into his eyes. Now he's the one holding back his tears. They aren't as bold as mine, but his sexy tan eyes shimmer with them.

"I love you, too. I think I always have."

He nods. "I feel the same way. We'll find a way to make this work, Amelia, we have to. Now that I've had you, I know I can't let you go." His arms tighten around me before he lightly dips his head down to kiss me.

One of his hands moves down my backside, the other plays with my breast, moving the nipple between his fingers with a light pressure.

"What if Haysleigh hates us for this?"

"She's my daughter, she's going to have to understand."

"What if she asks you to choose between us?"

Ryker stops kissing me and pulls away.

"I don't know," he answers hesitantly. "I love you with every beat of my heart, but she is my flesh and blood. Her happiness means everything to me."

I nod. "Maybe it's best if we stop this before we both get hurt."

He stares at me intently and sighs, "Maybe you're right." His hands drop to his sides and I instantly miss how they feel on my wet skin. "This was a mistake."

More tears start falling from my eyes. This time he doesn't wipe them away.

"It was," I lie.

Nothing about us feels like a mistake. My only mistake was the hidden agenda I had behind it at the beginning. Ryker has no idea that I started that fire so he could save me. He doesn't know that my initial plan was to use him to hurt Haysleigh. Now that he wants to end things, his rejection is like a dagger plunging into my chest.

"You should probably go," I tell him, pushing him towards the door weakly.

"Amelia," he starts, as he begins to turn away. "I meant what I said. I love you. It's going to be hard to shut off these feelings for you, but I know it's what's best for both of us."

"I love you, too," I choke out, biting my lip so I won't beg him to stay.

Ryker exits the shower depressed and upset. The second the door closes, I collapse to the ground. I break down, sobbing quietly into my knees and arms, hoping the shower can drown my sorrows.

What did I just do?

How am I going to forget what happened last night? How can I live without him when I know what it feels like to make love to him?

I can't.

It's just not possible.

I'm going to have to find somewhere else to go. The temptation is too high living with Ryker. I'll talk to June while at work, maybe she will let me stay with her until I can get back on my feet. I have to figure out something. There's no way I can live in this house anymore after knowing what it's like to have Ryker inside of me. My heart can't take the rejection. I love him too damn much to put myself through that kind of pain every day. If I can't be with him, then I need to leave him. It's the only way.

V. Kelly

"So, let me get this straight. You found your sleazy friend with your equally sleazy boyfriend fucking like dogs in your bed, then after you kick their asses out of your house you decided to burn all their shit in a fire."

"Bon voyage fire," I correct her.

"My bad, a *bon voyage* fire. A fire that you started because you were hoping that your friend's dad would come and extinguish it for you. Instead, you caught your grandmother's house on fire, almost died in the process, then your knight-in-shining-daddy-armor swoops in and rescues you right before your house explodes, brings you back to life with his kiss, and then you turn around and sleep with him to get revenge on his daughter."

"Right, but you forgot the part where I fell in love with him."

"That's right. You *fell in love* with the guy that you revenge fucked to piss off his daughter." She rolls her eyes. "You got some big cajones, my friend. Only someone with big fucking balls would seduce their best friend's dad for revenge. God, he's really thirty-seven? What the hell were you thinking? That's a huge age gap."

"The biggest."

"Well, are you going to tell me how he was in bed?" June questions, her smile wandering her face like a nomad looking for a home.

"Fuck. It was amazing. He was amazing. That man played my body like a god damn flute, touching every hole until our bodies united in this perfect melody that my body is still humming. It was by far the best sex I've ever had in my life." I can't stop smiling.

When June's eye raises in questioning approval, I feel my face flush.

She puts a hand to my forehead and grins, "Do you need some ice? Your face is so red, the customers are going to start complaining of how hot we keep it in here."

I swat her hand away and laugh, "We have no customers right now."

The coffee shop has been dead since noon, which is why I chose to talk to June now. We close the shop down in an hour.

"Do you think I can crash with you until I get on my feet?"

She shakes her head. "No can do, my friend. My apartment is being fumigated. I found a roach in my closet last week. Those things breed like rabbits. Where there's one roach, there are sure to be more. The entire building is being fumigated for them. We think the nasty couple that lives down the hall from me brought them into the building."

"Damn, you were my only hope of getting out of Ryker's house right now."

"Give me two weeks. If you still feel like you need to move out, you can have my guest bedroom, but we're splitting rent fifty-fifty."

"Of course."

A man stumbles into the coffee shop. He's moving around like he's drunk, bumping into chairs and tripping over nothing. He's wearing an oversized black hooded sweatshirt, baggy sweatpants, and a black beanie. He stares up at our menu, but he can barely read it through his half-opened eyes.

June walks over to the counter and greets him.

"Good afternoon, Sir, can I interest you in a cup of our famous Joe today?"

"Do you carry alcohol here?"

Both June and I share a look, the same look we get any time a customer wanders in with an outlandish request.

V. Kelly

"No, Sir, we only have coffee here," I reply sweetly.

The man looks over at me, blinking strangely like he didn't realize there were two employees working.

"What kind of bar doesn't serve fucking alcohol?" The man growls. He starts fidgeting and I suddenly feel uneasy.

"Well, Sir, this is a coffee shop, not a bar. We're also getting ready to close soon. If you would like a cup of coffee, I can get you one on the house."

"I don't want fucking coffee. I want alcohol, bitch. Actually no, fuck that, I want money. Give me all the fucking money in that register and your safe back there."

The man holds up a pistol and points it at June's face. "Did you hear me, bitch? Give me your fucking money."

June looks over at me, but we both are frozen in place.

"Hurry the fuck up!" he screams.

"Okay," June cries. She starts punching keys on the cash register but is so scared she keeps hitting the wrong ones.

"Are you trying to play games with me, bitch? I swear to God, I'll shoot you in your pale emo face."

His finger taps the trigger, and my stomach bottoms. June is shaking so hard she can barely stand upright.

"I … I … I don't know what's wrong. It's not working." She's so flustered that tears start streaking down her face, messing up her pretty dark makeup.

Underneath all her badass exterior is a girl who gets scared like everyone else. No amount of gothic makeup and spiky bangles can disguise her fear right now.

I carefully walk towards them with my hands raised above my head, making sure I do so in a non-threatening manner. I'm not sure what's giving me this sudden jolt of bravery, but maybe it has something to do with almost dying a week ago.

The man turns his gun on me. "What the fuck do you think you're doing?"

"She's scared. Let me help her. I'll get you your money and then you can go, just don't hurt us."

The man's eyes are wide, wild, and blood shot. They keep darting from side to side. I think he's on something.

He watches me as I walk over to June and move in front of her. She cowers behind me. If the guy shoots now, he's going to get me first.

I take a deep breath and punch the right keys on the register to open it. The drawer opens and I carefully pull out all the money, stuffing it into a brown bag we use for our baked goods.

"Now that one," he orders, pointing to the other register.

"That one is empty," I tell him. "We only keep one register open this close to closing time."

"You better not be lying to me. I'll fucking kill you!" He points the gun at my face, threatening me with it.

"The rest of the money is in our safe. Let me grab it for you." Near the safe is a panic button. The owner of the shop put it in when a slew of armed robberies started happening to businesses around us a few months ago. I wonder if this is connected in some way. Not that it matters. Right now, I'm only focused on getting out of here alive.

I can feel his eyes piercing my back, watching as I walk from the empty register to the safe. I crouch down, punch in the code to open it, then while I think he's not looking press the panic button hidden beneath the counter.

"What the hell did you just do?" He screams, obviously noticing me doing something I shouldn't have.

"I'm getting you your money," I quickly answer, unloading all that I can from the safe.

V. Kelly

He hops over the counter and marches over to me. His hand grabs my ponytail and jerks me back, throwing me into June's trembling arms.

He drops to one knee and looks under the counter. I swear my blood turns to ice when he turns his head like a vulture and those dangerous eyes bore into me. Death seems to be breathing down my neck lately. Why did I let him see me press that button?

He whips around and stomps towards us. He presses the gun to my head and sneers, "I told you not to play games with me, bitch. Now I'm going to have to kill you both."

I hold my breath, closing my eyes as he digs the tip of his pistol into my forehead. Then I feel the brute force of cold metal hitting me across the face as he takes his gun and connects it with my cheek.

June cries out, "Mia!" before he hits me again.

I hear something crack. Maybe a tooth. Maybe my jaw. Then everything goes numb.

"Stop hitting her!" June screams trying to protect me.

We hear sirens approaching the coffee shop and the man begins to panic. He grabs the bag of money, stuffing it with some of the money that's still inside the safe, before he hurls himself back over the counter.

We think that's the end of it, but then he turns around and looks me dead in the eye.

"Oh yeah, I almost forgot . . ." he points the gun at my face. A cold sneer creeps across his lips, right before I see his finger squeeze the trigger.

BAM!

Ryker

My mind keeps wandering back to my conversation with Amelia in the shower. *"What if she asks you to choose between us?"*

It was a question I didn't know the answer to. I'd like to think Haysleigh wouldn't force me to choose between her and Amelia, but she already tried to make me do that in my office the other day. Haysleigh asked me why I always sided with Amelia over her, and now I have my answer.

I love her.

I love Amelia.

The thought breaks me a little inside because of how we left things this morning. She didn't even say goodbye as she left for work. Now I can't stop thinking about her.

Did I make mistake agreeing to stop seeing her? It feels like a mistake. Thinking about living my life without Amelia makes me physically ill. I don't want to lose her.

"Yo, Ryker, you have an emergency call on line three." Lucius called out from the common area of the fire station.

Emergency?

My throat goes dry.

Did something happen to Haysleigh or Amelia?

I pick up the phone receiver and press the button to connect to line three.

"Fifth street fire station, Chief Thompson speaking."

"Ryker?" I hear Amelia sob into the phone.

V. Kelly

"Amelia? Is everything okay?"

"We were robbed," she cries.

"Robbed? What do you mean?" My hands slicken with sweat. It's obvious Amelia is okay, but I can hear the fear creating havoc in her voice.

"A man came into the shop. He was acting really weird. He started cussing out June, then he pulled a gun and asked us to empty the cash register. I tried to be brave and pushed the panic button, but he caught me doing it. He . . . he . . ." she breaks down into a wailing cry. "He hit me with his gun. Then he . . . he . . . shot at us."

My whole body goes incredibly still.

"Are you hurt?"

"Yes . . . no. It hurts where he hit me, but he was too drunk or high to aim the gun right. It hit the safe door and ricocheted into a nearby wall. Then the cops stormed the building and shot him. There's blood everywhere, Ryker. So much blood!"

"I'll be right there."

"You don't have to."

"I'LL BE RIGHT THERE," I shout into the receiver before hanging it up.

"Lucius, I need you to watch the station. I'll be back as soon as I can." I don't wait for him to answer me. I'm out the door and in my vehicle within a few seconds of leaving my office.

When I pull up to Amelia's work, there are cops everywhere. I slam my door and try to break through the crowd of people surrounding the building.

"Sir, I'm going to need you to step back." An officer I don't recognize tells me.

"It's okay, Canady, he's the fire chief and trained EMT. Let him through," Milton, the Chief of Police, tells his officer.

The officer eyes my outfit before stepping aside so I can get around him.

"Are you reporting to the scene?" Milton asks when I pause next to him.

"Not exactly. My daugh . . . no I mean my girl . . . well . . . someone I care about is inside."

Milton eyes me carefully, before leading me through the doors of the building.

A man's body is lying in the middle of the coffee shop. Blood is everywhere. It's on the chairs and splattered across the ceiling and walls. There's even a large pool of it circling his body.

"Our officers heard shots fired from inside. We stormed the building just in time. His first shot missed the two baristas working, but he had the gun aimed and ready to gun them down."

My eyelids squeeze together tightly as I try to suppress the image of the man shooting at Amelia and her friend. I see her standing over by the counter, holding another girl in her arms as they both sob together. I want to run over to her and check on her, but I don't.

"One of my officers fired off a warning shot and told him to put the gun down, but then he turned and fired at my officers. Took eleven shots to bring this bastard down."

"Eleven? Isn't that a little excessive?"

"Yes, but he kept moving, like he was some fucking zombie on steroids. I tell my officers to shoot to wound and only go for the kill shot when it's necessary. When the dude wouldn't stop shooting his gun, one of my deputies nailed him right between the eyes. It's a good thing he did, too. This mother fucker has robbed nine places of business in the last seven months, wounding at least five innocent people, and killing two."

V. Kelly

"Damn," I murmur, staring down at the man who tried to take Amelia away from me. If he was alive, I'd be strangling him with my bare hands, but since he's dead, I settle for clenching my fists instead.

"Ryker?" I hear Amelia cry. She runs across the room and stops just a few feet away from me when she notices the body on the ground.

"Don't look," I tell her, moving from the police chief's side and pulling her into my arms. She sobs hysterically into my shirt, clutching it with her shaking hands, as she fails miserably at holding herself together.

"I almost died again," she tells me. "It's like karma is trying to get back at me for all the bad things I've done."

I lift her chin, "Hey now, don't talk like that. We both know that you're not the kind of person that does bad things, Amelia." I cringe when I see the purple bruise on her forehead.

That damn asshole hit her, then he tried to kill her.

"But I have," she wails. "I burned my house to the ground. I slept with my best friend's dad." She says the last part in a hushed whisper. "And then I fell in love with him."

My heart melts.

"He fell in love with you, too," I tell her, lifting her chin to give her a quick kiss. I don't care who sees us. Almost losing her has made me realize that life is too short to hold back your feelings.

"You can take her home, if you want," Milton tells me. "A medic checked out her head wounds and says that she looks okay, but you may want to keep an eye on her. Head trauma is not something to take lightly. That mother-fucker hit her hard." Milton's brashness doesn't faze me, but it shocks the hell out of Amelia. She stares at him with a slightly slack jaw. When he catches her staring at him, he chuckles. "My apologies, Ma'am, Chief Thompson is used to my language, I forget to keep it reeled in when others are around."

"Do you think we can cover his body? At least until I get the girls out of here?"

"Sure. Mack, go get a cloth."

A deputy rushes out of the building and back in with a black cloth. He covers the body with it. I didn't realize Amelia had been holding her breath until she exhales beside me.

"Every time I look at him, I see his crazy eyes behind the gun barrel. A murderous look of rage mixed with a thirst for blood." She shivers. "I almost died again."

I grab her shoulders and pull her into me. "Let's get your friend and get out of here."

A man with long gray hair, small lensed glasses, bright green bohemian clothing, and sandals ambles up to us.

"My aura is quite black today, Mia. My spirit guides have blessed us all by protecting you and June." He grabs her shoulders and pulls her into a hug.

He smells like lavender and sage, I have to hold my breath, so I don't sneeze all over him.

"Thank you, Bodhi," she exclaims, "to you and your guides."

I roll my eyes. Amelia told me once how "alternative" her boss is, but if I hadn't seen him with my own two eyes, I wouldn't have believed her.

"Namaste," he says, bowing to me with his palms pressed together.

"Um, hi," I say, because I honestly don't know how to respond.

He frowns. "Your aura is very chaotic. You should really cleanse that." He pulls a hawk feather out of his pocket and starts brushing it around my shoulders. "No, this will not work at all." He takes out a lighter and thick chunk of bound wood and lights it.

"Yes. Yes. Very cleansing sage is." He twirls around me and Amelia, pushing the smoke from his sage stick towards our faces.

Amelia coughs.

I'm ready to punch him.

"There so much red energy surrounding you both. Turmoil, passion! Yes. Yes. Cleanse you both of this chaos." He stops in front of me and blows the sage in my face. "Free yourself of what binds you. Open your eyes to see what you really need."

My fists are clenched and ready to swing, but the second the smoke circles my face, a sudden wave of clarity washes through me. It could be a result from Amelia grabbing my hand and lacing her fingers in mine, but in that second, through a veil of white smoke, I could see my future, and in that future all I see is Amelia by my side.

I squeeze her hand; she squeezes it back.

"Take a few weeks off. I'm gonna close up shop up to do some renovations," he states eyeing the dead body on the floor. "Full cleanse for all this negative energy. I'll pay you of course. Consider this my compensation for the trauma that you and June have been through. Trauma can dampen your will to work, and I need you both to be at your best when I reopen the shop. I'm thinking yellow—a color of emotional joy and freedom. We will rid ourselves of these oppressing teal and gray walls and cleanse this place top to bottom. Negative entities be gone." Bodhi abruptly turns and grabs Amelia by the cheeks. After examining her face, he scrunches his nose. "Feel peace inside of yourself, Mia. I see dark things swirling around you. You need to figure out a way to cleanse yourself of these demons and forgive those who have hurt you."

Her eyes widen.

Bodhi drops the hold he has on her face and smiles. "Peace to both your hearts." He bows, before moving on to someone else.

"Well, he's interesting," I comment once he's out of ear shot.

Amelia giggles, "He's a trip to work with. Probably one of the most laid-back bosses I've ever had." Her face suddenly falls when a man walks in and uncovers the face of her assailant. She turns away from him and looks over at a wall, then she turns back to me when she realizes the wall is dripping in his blood.

"Let's get out of here. You've been through a lot today. It's time we get you home to somewhere safe."

She nods in agreement, but not before she rushes over to June to check on her. After they converse for a few minutes and Bodhi performs an impromptu cleansing on June as well, I end up escorting both girls outside.

June is still trembling but assures us that she's safe to drive home. I don't believe her. I could see the fear in her eyes, but I don't know her well enough to argue.

I hand Amelia my house keys and tell her to head back to the house. I don't want to leave her, but I still have a few hours of my shift that I need to fulfill.

"I don't want to be myself," she whispers.

"I know, baby, but I have to work. You'll be safe at my house, I promise. I'll be home in a few hours, then you won't be alone anymore."

She nods her head and fights some pesky tears that are pestering her eyes.

Before I know it, I have her in my arms and we're kissing, my fingers digging through her hair, her fingers clenching my back.

V. Kelly

I reluctantly pull out of her grasp, knowing that I can't prolong going back to work much longer.

"I'll see you soon, okay?"

"Okay," she whispers, before turning to climb into her car.

My heart breaks as I watch her leave. I'm glad she's safe, but I also don't want to leave her alone.

Amelia

It seems like eons before Ryker finally gets home. I've done a lot of thinking since he's been gone and realize that holding back my feelings is going to be more detrimental to my mental health than acting on them. Ryker showing up to my work, and then him holding me and kissing me, telling me everything is going to be okay, is exactly what I needed to work through everything that happened today.

I can't close my eyes without seeing that man with his gun: the barrel pointed straight at my face, and the brief closing of his eyes that actually saved my life. I remember watching the bullet fly at us in slow motion and flinching when the gunshot rang out, thinking to myself this is it; I'm going to die. The whole situation petrified me to the point I thought I was going to soil my pants. The relief I felt when the bullet hit the safe behind our heads and ricocheted in a different direction is something I will never forget, but there's one image I can't shake no matter how hard I try—his face—his dead, bloody face.

Sometimes I look at the walls and swear I see smatterings of blood all over them. I even see his dead body lying on the ground, gun a few feet away from him, his finger still curled like he just pulled the trigger.

Every little sound reminds me of a gunshot. The closing of a cupboard, the backfire of a beat-up truck outside. Every time I hear something that even remotely sounds like a shot, I fall to the floor and wrap myself up in a fetal position.

V. Kelly

That's the exact position Ryker finds me in when he gets home . . . curled up in a ball, tears streaming down my face, with nothing but panic in my eyes.

"Amelia?" he frowns when he finds me on the floor. He drops down beside me and scoops me into his arms. His fingers rake over my scalp, combing through my tangled blonde locks as he tries to soothe me. "I'm home now. Everything is going to be okay now that I'm here."

My fingers clutch onto his clothing, and I'm terrified of letting him go. I don't feel like talking. I don't feel anything but afraid. Holding Ryker helps me feel safer, it seems like his arms are the only thing that makes me feel safe anymore.

I look up and study him. His hair is matted to his forehead, sweaty from a hard day at work. His khaki colored eyes are shining with worry, and I know it's because I'm not talking. Right now, talking seems insignificant. The only thing that matters is feeling safe.

That slight smell of smoke permeates my nose as I nuzzle his shirt, but the smell doesn't bother me, it only makes me want to hold him tighter and longer.

"Come on, Amelia, let's get you to bed." Ryker's arms go beneath my legs as he lifts me off my feet. He carries me to the back bedrooms, passing by the guest bedroom and carrying me all the way to his instead.

I stare up at him with questions in my eyes, still not talking.

"I need to take a shower, but stay right here, I'll be back," he tells me before exiting the room.

I don't want him to leave, but I'm too weak to beg him to stay.

Ten minutes later he reappears, rubbing a towel against his wet head, while another is wrapped tightly around his waist. His muscles are glistening with beads of water specifically catching on the slats of his six-pack and the dangerous V that's dipping beneath his towel.

I nibble on my lip, unable to hide the burning desire coursing through my veins. He grins, it's extremely sexy and has my face heating up.

"So, I'm not gonna lie, seeing you vulnerable like this makes me want you."

He stalks towards me, dropping the towel as he goes. I watch him attentively, knowing damn well that this is exactly what I need to forget about my day.

"I've been doing some thinking," he states, crossing the covers on the bed. "Today, I almost lost you again. As I was driving over to the coffee shop, I realized that losing you would absolutely devastate me. I know we agreed to stop whatever is going on between us, but I don't think I can, Amelia. I'm in love with you. I've been in love with you for a very long time. I thought that us being together would be considered wrong, but I feel like not being together would be even worse. I don't like stuttering over what to call you. When Milton asked me why I was there today, I almost called you my daughter, but I almost called you my girlfriend, too. I don't like knowing what to call you anymore. I think it should be your decision on what your title is, because I already made my choice. I don't care what anyone thinks anymore, even Haysleigh, I want to be with you, Amelia, from this day forward."

His words are what I desperately need right now. Being with Ryker would make me the happiest woman in the world. He's the only man I can picture spending the rest of my life with.

"What about Haysleigh?" I whisper, because talking loudly seems like too much right now.

V. Kelly

"We'll have to break it to her gently. If we're going to be together, then it's important that we stay honest, especially with her. Hopefully, she will understand."

My bottom lip starts to quiver. Honesty. Something that I've been lacking since Ryker saved me from the fire. I probably should tell him the real reason I set that fire and reveal my hidden agenda for us, but now he's touching my cheek and I don't want to ruin this moment.

"Can I make love to you again?"

I careen my face, so my cheek brushes his palm. "I would love that."

He's at a disadvantage because I'm fully clothed and he's completely naked, so he grabs my shirt and pulls it over my head, revealing that I'm not wearing a bra. He smiles and lightly thumbs my nipples, playing with them as he moves in to kiss me.

The kiss starts out slow. His tongue invades my mouth, then he slightly nibbles as he tugs the bottom of my lip between his teeth. As we kiss, I feel his hands traveling up and down my sides until he hooks both of his thumbs onto my shorts and slides them down my body. Now I'm naked, because I wasn't wearing underwear, either.

"Naughty girl," he breathes, taking in every inch of my exposed skin. "If I didn't know any better; I'd say you were waiting for me."

I bite my lip. "Maybe a little."

He sort of growls as he climbs on top of me. I don't know why I feel find it so sexy, but I do. "You make it impossible to be good."

"That's okay; I like it when you're bad."

His mouth turns slightly upward, a confident smirk that compliments his handsome face.

I take my hand across his chin, tracing his stubble with my palm like it's a book of braille that will tell me all his secrets.

He climbs on top of me, spreading my legs wide so he has free access to his prize. I feel his dick enter me first. He does it slowly, pushing himself inside of me until every inch has disappeared. His lips come down next, moving in tandem with his hips as he slides slowly in and out of me. I arch my back, head digging into his pillow.

"Fuck, that feels good," I cry, when his pace starts increasing. My hands wander across the muscles of his back, feeling every hill until I have a firm grasp on his ass cheeks. I dig my fingers in and force him to take me harder.

"Careful. If you keep doing that, I'm going to finish too early. Tonight, I want to take my time with you."

And take his time he did.

For almost an hour we continue at this pace. It's slow and passionate and incredibly maddening. I want him to go faster, I even beg him for it, but he must have his reasons for going this painfully slow.

"Please, Ryker, a little faster."

He shakes his head and drags his lips and tongue down my neck, continuing his methodical and deliberate thrusts. My core is practically shaking. Every kiss, every touch, sends shock waves throughout my body, and it's then that I realize what he's doing.

The orgasm hits me hard. Like a silent assassin, it fires off all the nerves in my body at once. My fingers dig into his back then move up to his hair, pulling on the wet strands as I moan into his ear. He waits for me to finish, then begins moving faster.

It's not long before he shudders on top of me, his come warming my insides.

V. Kelly

"Fuck," he breathes. He has one hand on my hip the other is tangled in my hair, clutching it close to my scalp.

"Amazing," I gulp.

His eyes drift to mine and he smiles before kissing me with a few swift kisses to my mouth.

"You're going to be my undoing, Amelia. You've ruined me for all other women."

"If I have my way, you'll never need another woman ever again."

He grins, it's almost boy-like with how his eyes are gleaming, his smile stretching practically to his ears.

"I like the sound of that."

He's about to dive in for another kiss, when we hear keys in his front door.

"Oh shit! I think that's Haysleigh," he exclaims, jumping off me.

"What do we do?"

"I don't know," he breathes, running a frustrated hand through his hair. He grabs the towel off the floor and wraps it around himself. "Stay here, I'll see if I can get her to leave."

"Okay."

"Daaaaad! Are you here?" I hear Haysleigh yell from the living room.

My heart starts drumming in my chest—a furious beat of guilt, fear, and anger. Just hearing her voice makes me want to tear her apart for hurting me.

"I'll be right out, Haysleigh. I just got out of the shower." Ryker throws me a pained look and hops into a pair of loose black sweatpants before bolting out his door.

I wait five minutes, then carefully put on my clothes, knowing that if Haysleigh catches me in her dad's room everything will be over.

I creep out of the bedroom and slowly make my way across the hall, ducking into the guest bedroom before Haysleigh has a chance to see me.

I quietly shut the door and then take a deep breath.

Well, here goes nothing . . .

Ryker

I rush out of the bedroom in just my sweatpants, leaving Amelia naked and alone in my room.

"Haysleigh is standing in the living room, her hand intertwined with Willis who looks like he's about to faint.

Oh, hell no! Why the fuck is here?

"Daddy!" she says a little too sweetly. I see her drop Willis' hand and then fly across the living room into my arms.

"Hey, Honey." My eyes dart over to Willis, who nervously shifts from foot to foot. "Willis." My tone is anything but nice, and Haysleigh pulls out of my arms with a disapproving look on her face.

"Come on, Daddy, be nice," she says sternly. "Willis wanted to come over here and ask you something."

Is it possible for your blood to boil and go cold at the same time? Because it feels like a thick layer of *Icy Hot* is flashing under my skin.

"Mr. Thompson, so good to see you again," he mumbles, sticking out his hand for me to shake.

I look at it, but don't even bother shaking it. This kid is delusional if he thinks I'm going to touch him. He quickly retracts his hand and looks to Haysleigh for help.

She smiles and says, "Go on, silly, ask him."

I don't like where this is going.

"Mr. Thompson, I've been doing a lot of soul searching this past week, and after losing everything I owned, I realized that life is too short to waste time on trivial things like complicated relationships. That being said, I wanted to ask for your permission, to . . . you know . . . marry your daughter and stuff."

That's the fucking weakest proposition for my daughter's hand, that I've ever heard in my life. I look at my daughter, who flashes me a cheap-ass diamond engagement ring. I bet the kid found it in a Cracker Jack Box. Dipshit.

"No."

"But, Daaaaady," Haysleigh wails. "I love him."

I hear a door close in the hallway and I freeze.

Haysleigh looks at me strangely. She must've noticed the look of sheer panic in my eyes. I told Amelia to stay put, but it sounds like she has other plans.

"What was that?" Haysleigh asks.

Amelia appears a few seconds later, looking Haysleigh dead in the eyes, then glancing over at Willis who looks even more green than before.

"I hope I'm not interrupting anything," Amelia says, leaning against the wall.

"What the fuck is she doing here?" Haysleigh roars.

"She's staying with me. I gave her the guest bedroom until she can get back on her feet."

"You've got to be kidding me! That bitch is crazy, Dad. She lit her own house on fire, probably on purpose, too. How can you feel safe bringing her under your roof? I hope you hid all the matches and knives."

Amelia's eyes darken.

Oh no, shit is about to go down.

Amelia takes a deep breath. "Your sleaze is showing again, Haysleigh, you may want to get that checked out."

Haysleigh marches across the room and gets up in Amelia's face.

V. Kelly

"Listen here, Mia. I don't know what your plan is but dragging my dad into your games isn't going to happen. My dad's too nice to throw you out on your ass, but I have no problem taking out the trash for him."

"The only thing trashy in this room is you, Haysleaze."

Next thing I know, my daughter swings at Amelia's face, her fist connecting with Amelia's cheek. Amelia pushes her violently in the chest and both girls go flying across the room and over the side of my couch. They land hard on the ground and begin wrestling with each other.

"Bitch," Haysleigh screams.

"Slut," Amelia cries.

Fists start flying. Amelia kicks Haysleigh in the gut, then Haysleigh gets up and starts dragging a screaming Amelia across the floor by her hair, pulling and tugging on it violently, like she's trying to pull it out from the scalp. Amelia's nails dig into Haysleigh's forearm with enough force that Haysleigh finally drops the hold she has on Amelia's hair. This allows Amelia to grab Haysleigh's foot, pull it out from under her, and bring Haysleigh to the ground with a loud thud. Amelia maneuvers herself on top of Haysleigh and starts pummeling her with her fists.

"Whore," Amelia screams.

"Fuck you, bitch," Haysleigh yells, shielding her face from Amelia's punches.

I can't watch this anymore. I move in quickly and grab Amelia around the waist just as she gives Haysleigh a good punch right to the mouth. Blood appears on Haysleigh's bottom lip.

"I hate you," Amelia screams, as I pull her off Haysleigh.

Willis jumps in and grabs Haysleigh before she has a chance to swing back at Amelia.

"I wish you would've died in that fire," Haysleigh seethes. "The world would be better off if you weren't in it."

"That's enough," I roar, causing both girls to pause. "I'm sick of this crap. I get that Haysleigh hurt you, Amelia, and that you currently hate each other, but violence and bickering like teenagers is not the answer." I'm still holding Amelia, who's currently shaking with so much anger I can barely contain her. Tears are spilling down her face, and I wish I could wipe them away, but Haysleigh is here, and I don't think revealing our little secret right now is the best idea.

"Willis, take Haysleigh home."

"Seriously, Dad? You're going to pick that fucking pyromaniac over your own daughter?"

"I took Amelia in because she has nowhere else to go, the fact that you can't see past your feud and have a little empathy for her situation really disappoints me, Haysleigh."

Haysleigh frowns, "This is what I mean. You always take her side. I'm your daughter, and you're throwing me out of your house instead of Crazy Pants over there who lights shit on fire."

"Slut," Amelia growls.

"Yeah, I may be a fucking slut, Amelia, but at least I'm loved." Haysleigh holds up her hand and flashes the unimpressive ring at Amelia. "Look who got the ring, bitch, sure as shit wasn't your pathetic ass."

Haysleigh's blatant disregard for Amelia's feelings only makes me angrier.

"Haysleigh, go home. Amelia is staying with me until she gets back on her feet. If you can't handle that, then I suggest you don't come around here until you can act like a grown-up. As for

V. Kelly

you, I think you're a piece of shit, Willis. What you put these two girls through is inexcusable. As far as I'm concerned, you will never have my blessing to marry Haysleigh."

Haysleigh gasps, "Daddy, that's so unfair. Willis hasn't done anything wrong."

"Hmm, let me see. He fucked my best friend for two years and broke my heart. Pretty sure that he's done *something* wrong," Amelia retaliates.

"Jealous much," Haysleigh laughs. "Face it, Mia, you're never going to be important to anyone but yourself."

Not true. She's important to me; I'm just too spineless to say anything at the moment.

Amelia looks at me but averts her eyes when she holds my gaze for too long. She might be pissed off, but she knows telling Haysleigh would only lead to more violence.

"Well, I don't care what you think, Daddy. Willis and I are going to get married. We'll even elope if we have to. If you can't support our relationship, then I don't even want you at my wedding."

Walking Haysleigh down the aisle has been one of my lifelong dreams. For her to try and take that away from me, stings worse than the time she told me she hated me and wouldn't talk to me for five weeks.

I'm about to respond, but Amelia beats me to it.

"Listen up, Haysleigh. I don't care what you think of me, but to deprive your dad of something that important because of your selfishness is absolutely ridiculous. Your dad loves you. We both know how much he's been looking forward to walking you down the aisle. So, stop being a selfish bitch, and listen to him. Willis isn't a good guy. If he cheated on me, he'll cheat on you next."

Haysleigh glares at her. "That's because you can't satisfy a man. Willis is happy with me because I give him what he wants."

Amelia scoffs, "He wants a dog, Haysleigh. That asshole had you barking like a mother-fucking dog in bed."

"What?" I growl.

Haysleigh looks at a petrified Willis and then back at me. My fists are balled at my sides and I swear I feel the vein on my neck pulsing.

"You know what? I think it's time to go. Don't you, Willis?"

The douche doesn't say a word. He's too focused on my fists and the lack of space between us.

"We'll try to talk again when you're in a better mood, Daddy. I hope by that time you'll have taken out your trash." She eyes Amelia before rolling her eyes.

I can tell that Amelia wants to attack her again, but this time she keeps a level head and takes a deep breath instead.

Haysleigh smirks before quickly grabbing Willis' hand and pulling him outside.

The second the door closes, Amelia growls. "I'm really sorry about hitting her, Ryker, but she provoked me."

I agree that Haysleigh started most of their fight, but it's still hard to choose a side when the two girls I love most in this world are fighting like cats in an alley way.

"We should probably get to bed," I tell her, taking her hand.

She smiles down at my hand in hers and squeezes. Her blue eyes wander up my arms and stop when they get to mine. "I really am sorry," she whispers.

"It's all over now," I tell her. "Let's not dwell on it. We should go to bed."

"Do you think that tomorrow we can put out some flyers about Slinky?"

V. Kelly

I nod. "Already done, that's what I spent most of my day doing. Hopefully, we get a call soon."

She tugs my arm and brings me in for a much-needed hug. The tension in my shoulders slightly lessens the second I feel her arms wrap around me. Holding her is all I need to feel at peace.

"You're perfect," she exclaims, kissing my lips lightly. "How did I get so lucky?"

I shake my head, "No, Amelia, I'm the one who's lucky," I tell her, pulling hair out of her face. It's messy from the fight. Amelia didn't get it nearly as bad as Haysleigh did. It was hard for me to watch them fight like that, but I didn't know what to do. All I could do was pull them off of each other. Her face is still purple where the robber hit her, but there isn't a single scratch on her other than that.

She frowns but doesn't reply. I wish she would tell me what keeps making her so sad. It's like she's keeping something from me but is too afraid to tell me what it is.

Hopefully, I can get her to open herself up to me. If this relationship is going to work, she's going to have to be as honest and open with me as possible.

Amelia

I wake up tucked firmly against Ryker. His arm is draped protectively around my waist and his light snores are tickling my ears.

I can't believe what happened last night. I didn't mean to fight Haysleigh, but when she said that I was better off dead, I couldn't take her crap anymore. I lashed out, taking Haysleigh over the side of the couch.

Ryker didn't say a word after we went to bed. We didn't make love again either. Maybe he felt like he would be betraying his daughter if we did, or maybe he is having second thoughts about us. I wouldn't blame him if he did. Fighting with Haysleigh was a stupid move on my part, but it's hard to bite your tongue when a serpent strikes you below the belt.

Ryker's phone rings on the bedside table. I feel him stir against me and then groan in reluctance as he moves to answer it. It's seven in the morning, but it's also a Sunday—Ryker's day off.

"Hello?" Ryker says when he answers the phone.

"Really!" he exclaims sitting straight up in the bed, "That's amazing. Yeah, we can meet in about thirty minutes, does that work for you?"

I sit up and watch Ryker's face light up. Whoever he's talking to is making him very excited.

"Awesome, please send me the address and we will see you then." He quickly hangs up the phone and turns to face me.

V. Kelly

"Someone found Slinky! They want to meet in about thirty minutes."

Tears immediately form in my eyes. They are happy, relieved tears, because Slinky is alive! My cat. My best friend. The only thing I have left in this world that loves me unconditionally is alive!

"Are they sure it's him?"

"She seemed pretty sure, but let's not get our hopes up until we get there. We need to make sure she found the right cat. I didn't have pictures of him, I only described him off of what I remembered."

Slinky has very distinctive markings for a cat. He has a single black paw, which is a very interesting feature since he's an all gray cat. If someone passed him on the street, they'd probably think he stepped in black paint. He also has a small chunk missing from his left ear where a neighborhood dog got a hold of him.

"Did you put on the flyer that he has one black paw?"

"I did."

"What about the bite out of his ear?"

"That's on there, too. I made sure to describe him the best I could."

"Then it has to be him!" I cheer.

I grab his face and kiss him hard. I can feel him smiling against my lips. His arms circle my waist so he can pull me on top of him. We're both completely naked. It feels better to sleep with someone with no clothes on. I feel his cock twitch beneath me, then it easily slides inside of my pussy as I put each of my legs on the side of Ryker's body.

We start off slow. His fingers dig into my ass cheeks as he slowly guides my body along his shaft.

"Damn, you feel amazing," he breathes.

"Please don't stop," I whisper into his ear, moaning as his lips trail over the dangerous spot on my neck. He's barely brushing them against my skin, but they feel incredibly soft and hitting all the right nerves.

"I'm not stopping until you come."

With the way we're moving, I know it won't be long before I do finish. I find his ear lobe and tug it between my teeth.

He hisses and I feel his dick harden even more, which doesn't seem possible.

"Faster," I gasp.

His grip on my ass strengthens so he can quicken our pace.

Ryker claims my breasts with his mouth, running his warm tongue around my nipple. He looks up at me and coy flirtatious smile toys with his lips, "Do you like this?"

"Fuck, yes." My fingers dig into the bottom of his back, barely fitting around his fit torso.

"This feels way too good and I know I'm getting close, are you?"

"Maybe," I whisper, moaning as he does one incredibly hard thrust inside of me.

He starts moving even faster. It's hard to focus on one thing he's doing because this man has the hands of an octopus. It's like I can feel him all over my body. His mouth roves around my skin, tickling its way down my neck and over my breasts. His fingers bite into my ass cheeks as his dick slams inside of me. Then I feel one of his hands move to my front so he can slowly rub my clit. It's almost too slow, because he hits all the right nerves causing me to spontaneously orgasm. I scream his name, my fingers clenching and digging even harder into his back.

V. Kelly

It takes three hard thrusts for him to finish, but I can feel his come leak inside of me.

"Fuck!" I scream.

He smiles.

I grip his shoulders as he slowly slides in and out of me.

"I never asked," he whispers into my ear. "Are you protected?"

"It's kind of late to ask, isn't it? But I am on the pill," I inform him. "We're good."

Not that it would matter. If I somehow ended up pregnant, I would keep the baby. The baby would be a part of both me and Ryker, and that's something I would never give up.

He lets out a relieved sigh. "Thank God."

His response is unexpected.

"Would getting me pregnant be a bad thing?"

"No, but it probably wouldn't be the best thing to happen right now. We're still wading the waters of this relationship, Amelia. A baby would only complicate that. Don't get me wrong, if you did get pregnant, we'd make it work, but I'm not looking to knock you up right now."

"Then why fuck me without a condom?" I can't hide the disgust in my voice. I push myself off him and get up off the bed.

"I'm sorry, I should've thought about that before we started this."

"You should've thought about a lot of things."

I'm angry and I don't even know why. I guess it sort of sounds like he doesn't want a future with me. I'm okay to fuck, but not to have a kid with.

"Amelia, come here," he orders. His voice isn't authoritative, but it does make me look at him.

"Look, Ryker. I have major feelings for you, but to hear you say things like that makes me believe that you're only in this for sex."

He reaches out and grabs my wrist, pulling me down on the bed next to him. "You know that's not true."

"Then why would it be bad if I got pregnant? Don't you want a future with me?"

"I'm thirty-seven."

"So?"

"I'll be almost sixty by the time the kid graduated high school. That's a lot to take in, Amelia. Besides, we barely started this relationship and you're already talking about kids. Don't you think we should slow down?"

He has a point, but it still doesn't change the fact that he's basically saying he doesn't want any more kids. That's a big deal breaker for me. I want kids of my own someday. At least one.

"Hey, what's wrong?" he notices the disappointed look on my face.

"I want kids someday, Ryker. If you don't want more kids, then we probably should stop this before it gets too complicated. Not wanting kids is a deal breaker for me."

He stares at me for a few seconds before he speaks. "I didn't mean for it to sound like I never want to have kids again, I just don't know if I'm ready right now."

I breathe out in exasperation. This is supposed to be a great day and I'm ruining it by being whiny.

"I'm sorry. I'll stop talking about it."

Ryker moves some of my hair out of my face. I notice he does that a lot. "If you and I are going to be in a relationship, then it's important for you to tell me how you feel."

V. Kelly

He couldn't handle everything I'm feeling. I should tell him about the fire, but I chicken out.

"We should probably get ready. Where are we supposed to meet this person?"

Ryker checks his phone. "She texted me her address, it's not far from where your house is."

"Was," I correct him.

He nods while frowning. "Right. Was."

I get back up from the bed and begin throwing on some clothes.

"Amelia," he says, watching me attentively as I dress myself.

"Yeah?" I ask, after pulling up a pair of jeans.

He stares at me for a few seconds before shaking his head. "Never mind, it's not important. Let's get going."

We get to the woman's house and are immediately greeted by an army of cats that surround us. They meow and brush against our legs, and almost trip us as we make our way up the steps.

"Stupid fucking cats," Ryker grumbles as we settle in front of the door. "Did you see Slinky anywhere?"

I look around me and frown. "Nope."

Ryker looks frustrated, but he knocks on the door loudly.

A sweet old woman answers the door. She has whitish-blue hair and she's wearing an obnoxious yellow muu muu. She's got glasses on that look more like googles and has to adjust them when she opens the door. In her arms is a white fluffy cat with an incredibly grumpy face. It hisses when it sees us and jumps out of her arms.

"Oh, Gracie Lou, don't be like that. She rules the roost around here. She doesn't like outsiders." She adjusts her glasses again and blinks a few times like she's examining us.

My heart sinks. How can a woman who can barely see us correctly identify my cat?

I feel Ryker grab my hand and give it an encouraging squeeze. It's like he can read my thoughts.

"You must be Mortimer's owner," the old woman comments.

"Mortimer?" I question.

"They each have names," she replies, motioning to our feline audience. "That orange tabby is Chester. The orangish red thing over there is Crazy Eyes. Those twin white and black cats I call Mouse and Fish, they get picked on a lot. That big fluffy black thing over there is named Fluffle Butt, he hates his name." She starts pointing to the rest of the cats on the porch. "Lightning, Bonkers, Princess, Yak Yak the hairball king, Tinkerbell, Juice Box, shh he has a major bladder problem, Gigantor is the big fat blob sitting over in the rocking chair, Fidget is that twitchy thing jonesin' for cat nip, Stuart is the cat with a mustache, and finally we have Bob, the tiny little tripod hopping around here somewhere." A cute little yellow cat hops by us with only three legs. He's tiny, and a little banged up, but he seems to be getting around okay.

I stare at all the cats, wondering how this woman remembers all of their names.

"Mortimer showed up around here a week ago. He's got a thing for Princess. I'm pretty sure he knocked her up, too. Caught them going at it a few times. I got no time for kittens."

"Um, are you sure that this Mortimer is my cat?"

"Come inside." She motions for us to follow her, which we reluctantly do.

V. Kelly

"I had to catch him once I saw the flyer. We get a lot of strays around here, so I thought he was just another homeless cat.

That's not far from the truth. We have no home anymore.

"Anyway, after my dear friend Mable told me about your flyer, I just knew Mortimer had to belong to you." She walks over to the kitchen where a crate sits on the table. "He's definitely a lover, this one."

I peer inside the crate and see a familiar face.

"Meow," he greets.

"Slinky!" I shout as I open the crate. The cat looks genuinely happy to see me. He purrs the moment he's in my arms again.

Ryker is smiling like crazy.

"I'm guessing Mortimer is yours?"

"His name is Slinky, but yes, this is my cat." I rub Slinky behind the ears. He almost looks like he's smiling.

"Perfect! I'll take that reward money, please. This Old Lady has a date with Bingo tonight."

Confused, I look over at Ryker. "Reward Money?"

Ryker starts thumbing through his wallet and pulls out a hundred-dollar bill. "Here you go, Ma'am. We can't thank you enough for finding Slinky."

The woman greedily takes it and drops the money into her bra.

"I got no time for kittens. If Princess ends up getting knocked up, once they ween, you're taking them off my hands."

Ryker goes green. Damn, he really doesn't want to talk about babies right now.

"Well, hopefully she isn't pregnant," he remarks.

I begin carrying Slinky towards the door. "Thank you for finding my cat, Ma'am."

"You're welcome. You can call me Mabel," she replies.

"Wasn't your friend called Mabel, too?" Ryker asks.

"There are three of us old broads that frequent Bingo night named Mable. Mable one, that's me. Mable the great who's number two, and Mable the bitch she is Mable number three."

I try not to laugh over the third Mabel's name, but it's hard.

"Well, we should probably get going. Thank you again for finding Slinky."

"It was a pleasure doing business with you. Now if you excuse me, I think someone is supposed to show up to claim Fluffle Butt here in a few."

Ryker and I exchange a look.

The old woman smiles at us. "Gotta wait for those rewards to get offered." She hands me Slinky's collar that clearly says his name and has my phone number on it, before she winks at us and closes the door in our faces.

"I think that woman just swindled money out of you," I exclaim.

"I think you're right. At least we have Slinky back."

"We?"

He looks at me kinda funny and stops me just before we get into his car. "Yes, we. I'm in this for the long haul, Amelia. There isn't much you can do to get rid of me now. If you love Slinky, then I love him, too. We're in this together."

I smile at him, but underneath that smile is my conscience nagging me to tell him the truth.

"Ryker," I start, knowing this conversation is not going to be good.

"Yes, baby?"

He looks at me with all the love in the world, and I can't lose it. Not when I have nothing left. Ryker is the only support I have anymore, and if I tell him what really happened the night of the fire, I'll lose him.

V. Kelly

I can't lose him. He's the only person in this world that loves me anymore.

"Never mind. Let's get Slinky home, we probably should swing by the store and get some litter and supplies. All of his stuff is gone now."

Ryker nods, "We'll make a pit stop."

I reluctantly get in the car, clutching my cat for dear life. I hate keeping things from Ryker like this. I need to tell him about the fire as soon as possible, otherwise, it's gonna eat me alive.

Ryker

It's been almost three weeks since Amelia started living with me. Slinky has made himself right at home. His favorite place to sleep is in my hall closet. Amelia is supposed to start working again next week, but I'm worried about her. She seems worked up about everything. There are times when I think she wants to talk to me about stuff, but she always stops herself and says, "never mind".

I'm starting to hate that word.

She's received even more bad news this week. The insurance company denied her claim on the house and she did lose everything. No insurance money, no house. Everything she loved is gone now. The good news is that Willis did not press charges about her burning his stuff. It may have something to do with me threatening his life if he did, but I'd like to think he's a decent guy underneath all that slime ball.

I've barely talked to Haysleigh since the last time she came to my house. It's kind of unnerving. I've never gone this long without talking to her since she's moved out. There have been a couple times where I almost picked up my phone to call her, but I didn't follow through with it. She needs time to cool off and I'm hoping eventually she will come back around.

"You ready for dinner?" I call out, waiting for Amelia to get out of the bathroom.

I decided to take Amelia out for dinner tonight to celebrate her not being charged with arson. The judge is a personal friend of

V. Kelly

mine, and when I explained to him what happened, he decided to let her off with a warning and some community service. Sometimes it's good to have friends in high places.

"Almost," she yells.

Ten minutes later she appears in the living room, taking my breath with her. She's wearing a long silver dress that dips low in the back and front. She's wearing her hair down and has on some sparkly bangles and matching earrings.

"Fuck," I whisper. "You look amazing."

My dick stirs in my pants.

I told her to dress up because I was taking her somewhere nice. I did not expect her to look like this.

"Is it too much?" she asks, eyeing my dress slacks and button-up shirt.

"No, it's fucking perfect."

The past few weeks have been absolutely amazing, but this is the first time we are actually going out in public together. I've purposely tried to stay away from the public eye as much as possible because of Haysleigh, but tonight I don't give a fuck. I'm ready to announce to the world how much I care about this woman.

But first . . .

I march across the room and grab her forcefully, pulling her beautiful body against mine.

"Whoa there, Tiger. Careful with the merchandise," she says in a Brooklyn accent.

"Oh, I'm not going to be careful. I'm going to carry you over to that kitchen counter, hike up this fucking dress and take you before we leave."

She grins. "Don't threaten me with a good time."

I warned her. She squeals when I pick her up and carry her across the living room. I plop her down on the cold counter and pull up her dress. I move her cute little lace panties to the side, because I'm too turned on to take them off. I need to fuck her before my dick explodes.

I undo my belt and pull my pants down to my knees. I angle her so she's in the right position and then slam into her. Her lace panties rub along the side of my dick, but I couldn't care less. Right now, the only thing that matters is making love to this woman.

She moans loudly, and bends backward as I hit the spot she wants me to hit. It's like this every time we have sex. The closer we get to each other, the easier it gets to get each other off.

Her nails dig into my shoulders, her legs bouncing as they dangle over my arms. She leans back on the counter, opening herself even more to me.

"Don't stop," she screams. "I'm almost there."

I start playing with her clit, causing her pussy to clench my dick inside. When she does that, it makes it impossible to keep myself together.

"You fucking love that, don't you?" I whisper into her ear.

"Mmm Hmm," she mumbles, biting her lip.

"Tell me you love me."

"I love you," she yells.

"That's right. Yell it so the whole neighborhood can hear you, Amelia."

I'm about to explode inside of her when the unthinkable happens . . .

My front door swings open.

V. Kelly

"What the fuck?" Haysleigh screeches.

Amelia shoots up and both of us look over at Haysleigh with our mouths on the floor. She's standing in the doorway holding a box of chocolate chip cookies in one hand and Willis' hand in the other.

I quickly pull up my pants as Amelia closes her legs.

"What the fuck is going on?" Haysleigh demands.

"Haysleigh, I can explain," I start.

Haysleigh looks appalled. "Please don't tell me that you're so desperate for attention that you've resulted to fucking my dad, Mia. Fuck, I knew you were a slut, but damn you're really fucked up in the head. God, you're a sick bitch."

"Haysleigh, that's not fair," I scold. "Amelia and I didn't mean for this to happen, but it did."

"What to happen? Sex. She's a fucking deranged, pyromaniac slut, she definitely meant for this to happen."

Amelia jumps off the counter and smooths down her pretty dress. Willis actually looks hurt that they caught us together. That asshole has no reason to be hurt; not if he's planning on marrying my daughter. Which will never happen as long as I'm living.

"Haysleigh, I know this looks really bad, but I can assure you that my feelings for your dad are genuine," Amelia explains. "I love him."

Haysleigh laughs, but it's full of mockery. "Fuck you, Amelia. I can't believe you're this desperate. I know you were pissed off when you found out about me and Willis, but I never thought you'd stoop to this level. Fucking my dad is an all-time low, even for someone as slutty as you."

"I'm not a slut," Amelia yells. "If anyone is a slut, it's you."

Haysleigh laughs. "Revenge is a bitch, isn't it, Whore? You're just mad that I had the last laugh. You have nothing now. You can fuck my dad and act like it means something to you, but we both know that you're a psychopath who only cares about herself."

"Now, Haysleigh, I know that you're upset, but attacking Amelia isn't going to help the situation. Why don't we talk this out like adults?"

"You're my dad! You aren't supposed to fuck my friends. How long has this shit been going on?"

"Since she started living with me."

"You both are sick. Especially you, Amelia. You need therapy. This shit is sick and wrong on so many levels. He's old enough to be your fucking dad."

"But he's not my dad! I love him."

"Bullshit."

"I do. Who are you to judge who I love? You had no problem sleeping with my boyfriend behind my back and falling in love with him."

"And he loved every second of it, too. You know how many times we laughed at you, Amelia? We used to fuck while you were asleep in the next room. He ate me out on the couch while you slept in the recliner next to us. We took pictures of us fucking while you slept. It was a joke. Your whole life is a joke. Nobody loves you, Amelia. Not really. You're a pathetic bitch who has nobody in this world, so you cling to people, making them think that they love you. My dad just felt sorry for you. You're nothing more than a pity fuck to him." Haysleigh is seething. Every angry word that spits out of her mouth is like a flying dart, ready to strike the bullseye of Amelia's fragile heart.

I see it breaking her apart, and I'm doing my best to try to deflect Haysleigh's rage, but I don't know how to make this better without making it worse.

So much for having a romantic night out together.

"Haysleigh, you really need to stop talking to Amelia that way. You're being vicious."

"I'm only saying what we all know is true. I don't know what she did to convince you to fuck her, Dad, but she's manipulating you. Is this her payment for letting her stay here? She stays here and you get to fuck her disease infested cooch anytime you want?"

"HAYSLEIGH, THAT'S ENOUGH!" I shout.

Haysleigh grins as she watches Amelia break down. Amelia's fists ball up against her sides as tears streak down her face.

"Fuck you, Haysleigh."

"What? Can't take it, bitch? Face it, you'll never be better than me. I've taken everything away from you, and now you have nothing but a whore reputation and a fucking record for being an arsonist. Way to pick 'em, Dad. Didn't know you were into felons."

"Haysleigh, you have no room to talk. You hurt me by sleeping with Willis all because you wanted revenge for something that happened in high school. Wasn't it you that said that you can't help who you fall in love with? Well, I've fallen in love with your dad. I can't help it, it just happened. Maybe, I've been in love with him for a long time, but that doesn't matter. What matters is that we want to be together."

Haysleigh's smile turns even more evil.

"Oh yeah, bitch, I got my fucking revenge. I get it every night while your ex-boyfriend's dick is fucking the shit out of my pussy. You were never enough for him. You'll never be enough for anyone, Amelia. You're not good enough for Willis. You weren't good enough for Hector, and you sure as shit ain't good enough for my dad."

"HAYSLEIGH," I scream. "Stop this right now."

"No, Dad. She needs to know her place, and her place is not in my family."

But her place is in this family. Her place is with me.

I'm about to open my mouth to say just that, when Amelia speaks one last time.

"You keep talking about revenge and how you've had the last laugh, Haysleigh. Well, I purposely lit my own house on fire just so I could seduce and fuck your dad. How's that for the ultimate revenge?"

And that's when the room goes silent.

Amelia

"Well, I purposely lit my own house on fire just so I could seduce and fuck your dad. How's that for the ultimate revenge?" The words fly out of my mouth with enough venom to slay a dragon. Immediately, I want to shove each one of those words back into my mouth and swallow them.

Why did I just say that?

This is not how I wanted to tell Ryker my secret, but now it's out there and I can't take the words back. I didn't fuck her dad, I made love to him.

Oh my god, I've ruined everything.

Haysleigh has gotten me so riled up that I said the first thing that popped into my head because I knew that it would hurt her, and I would win. Now, I can't erase the look of betrayal in Ryker's eyes.

"Is that what this was?" he rages, his eyes flashing with so much disappointment and hurt that it eats away my soul like acid. "Was I just some revenge fuck so you could get back at my daughter? Did you have this planned from the beginning?"

"No," I cry, flying across the room to him. "I didn't mean to say that. Our relationship is everything to me. You are everything to me." I grasp his arm and try to get him to look me in the eyes, but he won't.

He rips his arm out of my hands, his eyes boring into me with so much rage and disappointment that I can practically feel it searing through my skin.

I look over at Haysleigh, who's smiling triumphantly.

"See, Dad, I told you she was a whore."

"Fuck you, Haysleigh."

"No, Amelia, fuck you." She punctuates each word with a vicious smile and both of her middle fingers raised high into the air.

"That's enough! Both of you get the fuck out of my house."

"Ryker, please let me explain," I plead, clutching his arm again. "I may have started the fire with the intention to seduce you, but after I got here everything changed. I didn't want revenge anymore, I wanted you."

His glare intensifies, "Tonight, I think you've made your intentions very clear. You're a very selfish person, Mia. Only someone who is selfish, would use another person to get back at someone else. You got your revenge fuck like you wanted, you played with my heart like a ripped-up ball of yarn, and now you can get the fuck out of my house. I don't want to look at you anymore, both of you are children who need to do a lot of growing up."

"Ryker, please."

Tears are spilling down both of our faces, but he's too angry to listen to me, and I know that the damage is done.

"Daddy, it's okay. At least you know who she really is. I tried to tell you. Next time you should listen to me."

Ryker turns towards Haysleigh, his eyes wild and angry. "I know who both of you are now. You can stand there and beg me to accept this stupid piece of shit standing next to you, all you want, but he will never be a part of my family. He's toxic, Haysleigh. Look at what you've become! You were never this malicious, and now I don't even know how to look at you without feeling disappointed. This isn't how you should be living your life, Haysleigh. He doesn't deserve either one of you."

"Daddy, I told you that I love him. We're going to get married. I don't care how you feel about him, our love is eternal."

"If you marry him, don't bother coming back here."

Haysleigh looks appalled.

"You fuck up my relationship, I fuck up yours. How's that for revenge? Now get the fuck out of my house. We're done here," he growls.

I stand there like a statue. I can't take back what I said, but I also can't beg for forgiveness. Watching Ryker walk away from me shatters every emotion inside of me. I run after him, crumpling to the ground near his feet. I reach up and clutch the leg of his slacks. "Ryker, please don't leave me. I love you. I need you." I begin sobbing, holding onto his pants even tighter when I realize if he takes another step it's over—all of this will be over.

"Get out of my house, Mia. I don't ever want to see you again."

Mia... why is he calling me Mia? I'm Amelia to him. I'm his Amelia. No. No. No. Call me Amelia again. I need to hear you say my name.

"Ryker, I love you."

He looks down at me with hollow eyes, void of any emotion other than betrayal and anger. I can't tell if his tears are angry or filled with sorrow. He shakes me off his leg like I'm some stray dog trying to hump him, and stomps into his bedroom, slamming the door behind him.

"RYKER!" I screech.

I hear Haysleigh snickering behind me, I whirl around, completely livid and ready to pounce.

"Go ahead and fight me, Mia. Where's that gonna get you? My daddy will eventually forgive me because he loves me. You're nothing more than a whore who used him. He never loved you, not really. That's why he will never forgive you."

"Fuck you, Haysleigh."

"No, fuck you, Mia. Just remember who it was that got the last laugh, tonight. It sure as hell wasn't your pathetic whore ass." She cackles manically as she links arms with Willis. "Come on, Willis. Let's get out of here so the trash can take itself out."

Then they leave me.

Everyone always leaves me.

I can't believe this is happening. Tonight was supposed to be a celebration that I didn't get put in jail. Instead, it erupted into chaos, sentencing me to an even more eternal prison sentence— loneliness. I ruined everything. Why couldn't I just keep my big mouth shut? Why did I let Haysleigh get the best of me?

I can barely pick myself up off the floor, as I take the ultimate walk of shame back to Ryker's guest bedroom. I don't have much to pack, but every time I slam another thing into my bag, my heart breaks a little more.

I want to march into Ryker's room and demand him to talk to me, but I can hear him crying, and I can't face him like that.

I broke him.

I didn't mean to, but that's exactly what I did.

Haysleigh's right. I don't deserve Ryker. Hell, I don't deserve anyone. I'm pathetic. And pathetic, unloved humans don't belong in this world. Why didn't I die? I should've never survived that fire, or the shooting, but I did. And instead of finding my happiness, I've found my misery.

V. Kelly

Good job, Amelia. You really fucked this one up.

I throw a quick text to June to see if I can stay with her. When she says yes, I grab all my stuff and put it in my car.

As I walk back inside to grab my cat, I see Ryker emerge from his bedroom. He stops in the hallway but refuses to look up at me.

I open my mouth to say something but stop myself. I pick up Slinky from off the couch and start walking towards the open front door. I'm about to cross the threshold when I decide that I need to say one last thing to Ryker before I leave.

"For what it's worth, thank you for letting me stay with you. You were the only person who was there for me when everything in my life imploded and that's something I will never forget. I know you don't believe me, but I really do love you, Ryker. I didn't mean to hurt you. You mean everything to me. I never deserved your kindness, but you gave it to me anyway. I'm going to hold on to that, because that's all I have left now. I need to hold on to these memories because only one man has ever truly cared about me, and that's you. I will always love you, Ryker—probably always will until my last dying breath. Those words probably mean nothing to you, but I needed to get them out."

He doesn't say a word.

It takes everything I have to not drop my cat and run back over to him, pleading for his forgiveness. But I know I can't. The damage is done. He hates me, and all I can do now is walk out the door and leave peacefully.

I owe him at least that.

I take a deep breath and do the hardest thing I've ever had to do.

I turn around and walk away from the only man I have ever truly loved.

Ryker

Everything has been an absolute mess since I had my fight with Amelia. I feel sick. I can't eat. I can't sleep. I don't want to believe she used me for revenge against my own daughter, but she did. She purposely used me to get back at Haysleigh. Who does that? Haysleigh was right about one thing, Amelia is crazy. Only a crazy person would light their house on fire so that their best friend's dad will swoop in and save them. I was nothing more than a pawn in her fucked up game of revenge. The sad part is that the betrayal I feel is nothing compared to the misery of lying in an empty bed without her.

I let my guard down and fell in love with her—a helpless victim to a set of pretty blue eyes and full pouty lips. I still find pieces of her blonde hair in my bed, and I'd be lying if I didn't admit that sometimes I hold them over my heart, fighting the tears that want to fall down my face.

I've been so fucked up that I can't even focus. Being at work has been miserable. Everyone notices how off my game I am, but nobody seems to say anything. I work to get Amelia off my mind, but I can't help wondering if she's okay. I know she's staying with June, but I can't stop thinking about her. Every time I see a pretty girl walk by with blonde hair, my heart speeds up.

I don't know why I even care.

She betrayed me.

She used me.

I shouldn't love her . . . but I do. So much.

V. Kelly

I have a mountain of paperwork on my desk and I don't have the heart to do any of it. Nothing seems to matter anymore. Life isn't the same without Amelia in it.

I've thought about calling her to apologize, but I know that if I do that, I'll be falling into her trap again. She's like a black widow. Lures you in with her pretty colors and then devours you when she tangles you up in her web of lies. I'm just going to have to get over her. She hurt me and loving her shouldn't outweigh that—it can't outweigh that. I have to be stronger about this and stop acting so weak. I lived through the drama with Haysleigh's mom, I should be able to go on with my life without thinking about a twenty-one-year-old girl that broke my heart.

I can remember the exact moment where my feelings for Amelia changed. She was seventeen, almost legal, but still off-limits. I had a really hard day at work and came home extremely emotional. Haysleigh was too busy being self-absorbed to notice how distraught I was, but Amelia noticed right off the bat. She found me in my bedroom crying into my hands.

"What's wrong, Ryker?" Amelia asks from my doorway.

I looked up at her with tears streaming down my face, unable to speak. That day we lost a whole family to a fire. I tried to save a three-year-old boy from the blaze, but I couldn't get to him in time. I watched the ceiling collapse on top of him, his desperate cries still haunting my thoughts. Losing people like that, especially kids, always gets to me. I did everything I could to save that family, but I couldn't be their hero that day. I had to watch them die—that little boy lost his life because I couldn't save him.

"Hard day at work," I choke out.

She takes a cautious step into the room, then carefully walks over to the bed, sitting down beside me.

"Want to talk about it?"

I looked over at her, barely able to focus on her exquisite face through my tears. She was so young then. Naïve and innocent, but always so beautiful.

"We had a nasty fire today. We lost a whole family to it. I tried to save a little boy, but the roof collapsed over the top of him and I couldn't save him. I watched him die, Amelia. That poor kid never stood a chance."

I hung my head in defeat, feeling broken and hopeless. I squeezed my hands together, hoping that the pain of my fingers digging into my palms would help drown out the screams of that kid echoing in my head.

I felt the softness of her skin first as she draped her hand over the top of mine. Then I felt the protection of her fingers as she worked them into the spaces of my hands, prying them apart. She took my hand and placed it in her lap, holding it tightly as my body lightly shook between sobs.

"Ryker, you tried to save him and that's all that matters. You are the most heroic man that I know. I know you did everything in your power to save that family and that little boy. Don't beat yourself up over this, you're still a hero because you tried. You didn't give up. You put your own life in danger to save someone else. That's why you're a hero. If you could've saved that boy, you would have."

My eyes wandered up to hers. It was the first time I had ever been desperate to kiss her. I wanted to show her how much I appreciated her kind words and support. My own daughter couldn't even be bothered by me. I could hear Haysleigh down the hall, talking a mile a minute on her phone, probably to a boy. But Amelia sat next to me, holding my hand, telling me all the words I needed to hear in that moment. She let me cry on her

V. Kelly

shoulder. At one point, my head ended up in her lap. There was nothing sexual between us then, but the emotions were there— raw and filled with an unexplainable chemistry that scared the shit out of me. I had to suppress what I was feeling for her, but I didn't move away. I let her run her fingers through my hair, never saying anything as I wept in her arms. She didn't make me feel stupid for being a grown ass man weeping like a baby. She made me feel loved, accepted, and cared for. All the things I needed at the time. Sometimes I wonder if things would've turned out differently if Haysleigh had been the one to enter my room that day instead of Amelia. Would I still have fallen in love with her if she hadn't consoled me that day?

That was the exact moment I fell in love with Amelia Morris. From that day forward, everything changed between us. Now we're here, and I can't shake that day out of my head. I still love her even though she used me.

"Ugh," I groan, throwing my head on my desk. "Why is life so fucking hard?"

I'm about to pick up a stack of paperwork and attempt to work on it when the siren goes off in the station.

"Fire on fiftieth and Pine," Leroy shouts as he passes by my office. "It's an apartment building and dispatch says people are trapped inside."

I'd like to say that I spring up and immediately rush after him, but I don't. My body is too depressed to move swiftly. I reluctantly get up and drag my sulking body out of the office, following my guys to the truck.

"Boss, are you okay?" Leroy asks when I climb into the passenger seat.

"I'm fine," I tell him, throwing on my hat. "Let's go."

The ride to the fire seems to take forever. The entire time my mind is wandering back to Amelia's eyes, pleading for me to listen to her and forgive her for what she said. I can't forgive her. She said it plain as day. She was only using me to get her revenge on Haysleigh. She never loved me—not like I love her.

Leroy shakes my shoulder, "Boss, are you coming?"

I look up and see that we're parked in front of the building. Flames are roaring out the third-story windows. There is screaming and crying coming from the floor above it.

"We need to get in there and save those people," I yell, quickly snapping back into reality. I throw on my mask and instruct my guys to grab the hose as I enter the building gloved up and holding my pick head axe.

The bottom half of the building is filled with smoke. I see a woman come bumbling down the stairs, covering her head with a blanket. She looks to be in her mid-thirties, with long black hair and mocha colored skin.

"There's people on the fourth floor still. I don't think they can get out because their apartment is right above the one on fire," she coughs.

She runs towards the door and straight into Leroy's arms. He guides her outside while I start ascending the stairs. Usual protocol is to use a buddy system, but if people are in danger, I don't have time to wait for Leroy or Lucius to get up here.

I take the stairs two at a time and stop briefly on the third floor. The fire is raging outside the third-floor door. It looks as though everyone on that floor has been already rescued, but I can hear a child crying somewhere above me. I quickly spring into action, ascending the next flight of stairs until I'm bursting through the fourth-floor door. The hallway is filled with a thick

V. Kelly

smoke. I can barely see through my mask as I make my way deeper down the hall.

"Somebody please help us," I hear someone cry up ahead. As I make my way down the hall, I notice that flames are coming up through the floorboards, just before the last apartment. I see a young Asian girl and her mother peeking out from their apartment door, coughing like crazy.

"Hold on, I'm coming," I shout. The gap between their apartment and where I'm standing will be a hard jump, but somehow, I manage to leap across it and enter their apartment.

The apartment is filled with smoke, and I know that if I don't get them out of here, they're going to die. I look around and see that the woman has a long wooden shelf that stretches the length of one of her walls. I use the end of my axe and pry it from the wall, it's about the length we would need to get them safely across the gap.

I open their apartment door, carrying the shelf with me. Leroy is standing on the other side of the gap, and a sense of relief washes over me. This board would not hold my weight, but it can probably hold the woman's. I toss the wood across the gap and it barely clears the other side.

"Hurry," Leroy screams through his mask. "The sprinklers failed, and it looks like this whole floor is going to be gone soon. We need to hurry."

"Can you walk?" I ask the mother, who's doubled over and crawling across the ground.

"I can try," she coughs.

I grab the little girl and tuck her into me. She's probably eight or nine. "Sweetie, I need you to hold on to me, okay?"

She's clearly afraid and clutches onto my jacket for support.

"Don't be afraid, I got you."

I direct the woman out the door and tell her to cross the gap using the shelf as her bridge. She looks reluctant. The fire is licking up the walls and engulfing the sides of the board.

"We don't have much time. Go!" I order.

The woman looks back at her daughter before she puts a cautious foot on the wood.

"Come on, Lady, I got you," Leroy tells her.

It's not a big gap, but it's definitely daunting. I watch the woman take a deep breath, then she carefully crosses the board, almost losing her balance when the shelf starts to bow in the middle. Leroy holds the wood firmly down, and when the woman is close enough, he grabs her hand, pulling her to safety.

"Mommy!" The little girl cries.

"It's okay, we got this," I tell her, holding her even tighter. She kind of reminds me of Haysleigh when she was about her age. Thinking about Haysleigh only makes me more determined to save this girl's life. I know that the board can't hold my weight, but I also know that I can't jump the gap anymore, because more of the floor disappears into the floor below, the board barely hanging on to the other side.

"Ryker, hurry! You don't have much time."

I take a deep breath and run towards the board. My foot catches the beam and I make three long strides across it before I feel the wood breaking beneath my feet. I only have enough time to throw the girl at Leroy, who barely catches her before the wood gives out and I go tumbling through the floor.

"RYKER NO!" I hear Leroy scream, but it's too late. I fall backward, my body hurling down into the hungry fire that awaits me below.

Amelia

I've been violently ill for days. June seems to think I've caught the flu bug going around, and I'm starting to think she's right. I can't keep anything down, and the nausea is killing me. I haven't thrown up this much in a very long time. I think I might have a fever, too, but the sweat dripping down my face could also be a result of all the vomiting I've been doing.

Losing Ryker devastated me. Granted, I brought this on myself, but life seems incomplete now that he's gone. Sometimes at night I think I feel him lying next to me, until I realize it's June's giant cat, Lurch, who's seeking out my body warmth. I'm convinced this illness is just life's way of kicking me while I'm down. Flu season really sucks.

June finally decides it's time for me to go to the hospital when she finds me on the bathroom floor curled up in a ball next her toilet.

"That's it. I'm taking you to the hospital."

"I feel fine," I lie. I hate hospitals. The last thing I want to do is go to the hospital.

June sees right through my shit and shakes her head, "Bullshit! When was the last time you ate something? Fuck this self-pity starvation shit that you're doing. I'm taking you to the hospital and there's nothing you can do about it."

She helps me to my feet and walks me straight out the door. When June sets her mind to something, there's no arguing with her. That's why I don't try to talk her out of it when she places me in her passenger seat and rushes me to the hospital.

It doesn't take us long to get there, but they make us wait almost three hours before a doctor has time to see me. While we're sitting there, I overhear a nurse say that there was a big fire on the other side of town and that a few people were seriously injured.

What if one of those people injured was Ryker?

The thought rushes into my mind, causing my stomach to lurch again, this time with a tremendous amount of worry. I grab a bright blue vomit bag and dry heave into it. Nothing but spit comes out. I think I already threw up everything that was in my system.

"Amelia?" I look up and see a familiar looking nurse standing in a doorway. I quickly realize that it's nurse Jessica who helped me the last time I was here.

She frowns when she sees me weakly pull myself out of the chair. "Hey, I know you. Wait, are you the patient or are you here to see your dad?"

"My dad?"

"Yeah, that hot one that's not really your dad. They brought him in a couple hours ago. He's in ICU."

My heart literally stops beating in my chest.

"What do you mean?"

"He was hurt in a fire. He fell through the floor or something. He's been unconscious since he got here."

"Oh my god!" I cry.

I need to see him now!

I try to move faster than my body will let me and end up collapsing to the ground, hitting my head on a nearby chair.

V. Kelly

"Oh, no you don't," Nurse Jessica says, helping me to my feet. "You're going to a room. Let's get you checked out by a doctor first."

How can I possibly get checked out by a doctor when I know that Ryker is over in ICU fighting for his life? My illness doesn't matter right now. All that matters is Ryker.

My head starts to feel fuzzy and I barely feel Nurse Jessica plop me down in a wheelchair and wheel me to a back room. I don't wake up until the doctor arrives twenty minutes later.

When I finally open my eyes, I see him standing over me, smiling. "Why hello there, Amelia. I'm Dr. North. I must say, you gave us quite a scare back there. We got some fluids going through your IV. We also took some of your blood, we should have your results back in a few minutes, but my guess is that you're dehydrated. Your friend told us that you haven't been eating lately. Is that true?"

I nod. "I can't seem to keep anything down."

"The flu is pretty bad this year. I'll check your blood work and if that doesn't come back with anything then I'll have them swab your nose for the flu. Sound okay?"

"Not really, but okay. I have a question though."

"Shoot," he says smiling.

"I have a friend in ICU, can I go see him?"

He frowns. "No, not until we figure out what's going on with you."

"Oh, okay." Worry takes over my body again.

What happens if Ryker dies in ICU and I don't get to see him? The thought is like poison for my mind. I feel instantly weakened by it, regretting every single thing I did to lead up to this point in my life.

June walks in a few seconds later holding a cup of coffee. "Oh, good, you're awake," she exclaims, plopping into the seat beside me. "For a second there you looked dead." She takes a sip of the coffee and grimaces. "Ugh, this coffee tastes like camel spit." She places the cup on the table next to my bed and smiles.

I glare at her because joking about death when someone I love is possibly dying nearby is cruel.

"Uh oh, what's wrong?"

"Ryker's in ICU," I tell her. A single tear slides down my face. "They won't let me see him." I wonder if Haysleigh knows about her dad being in the hospital. Part of me wants to call her, but the other part of me is hesitant.

"Well, when you faint and take a header in the lobby, yeah, they aren't going to let you go anywhere."

"True. Hey, can you hand me my phone? It's in my purse."

"Sure," she says, grabbing it out of my purse and bringing it over to me.

I quickly open it and find Haysleigh's name, she's currently labeled "slutopotamus" in the directory.

Me: Hey, I'm not sure if you know this yet or not, but your dad is in the hospital. He's in ICU.

I see the bouncing three dots as she types out a response.

Slutopotamus: What the fuck do you mean my dad is in the hospital? What the hell did you do to him?

Bitch.

Me: I didn't do anything. The nurse told me there was a fire and he got hurt. It has to be bad because he's in ICU.

Slutopotamus: Shit. Shit. Shit. I'm nowhere near town right now. I'm actually in Las Vegas. Is he okay? Why are you the one contacting me? Shouldn't the hospital be calling

V. Kelly

me? Why do you even care about him? I thought you two were done with your disgusting relationship.

What the hell is she doing in Vegas? Why am I even worrying about that right now? The only thing that matters is someone being here for Ryker. I'm not going to let her mean digs get to me.

Me: We are . . . I'm in the hospital with possible flu symptoms. The nurse remembered me from when I was last here, and that your dad visited me. That's how I found out. I haven't even seen him, yet.

Slutopotamus: Stay away from him. He doesn't need your negativity surrounding him.

Me: Haysleigh, if you're in Vegas, then somebody needs to be here for him.

Slutopotamus: I'll be on the first plane I can to get there. Just stay away from him.

Me: Make me. He needs someone here and I don't plan on leaving him. I'll be here as long as he's here, even if I have to wait in the lobby the whole time.

I see the three dots bouncing again before they stop. Then they start to bounce again, this time for a shorter amount of time.

Slutopotamus: Fine. I'll be there as soon as I can.

I decide not to respond, even though I find her lack of urgency annoying. I'd give anything to be in Ryker's room right now. I'd hold his hand and tell him that I'm there and everything will be okay, just like did for me. Haysleigh has to be the most selfish person I've ever met. Who chooses to stay in Vegas when their dad is possibly dying in the hospital? Damn this hospital. Damn them for making me stay in this shitty emergency room while Ryker's suffering in ICU.

Nurse Jessica pops into my room, all smiles. "Is somebody ready for their flu test?" she asks sweetly, even though there's nothing sweet about a flu test.

"Ready as I'll ever be. The sooner you get it done, the sooner I can rush to ICU and check on Ryker."

She nods and grabs a gigantic Q-Tip and unwraps it from its package.

"Eww, I'm out," June tells me. "I hate watching these things go up people's noses." She leaves the room in a hurry, just as Nurse Jessica attempts to shove that Q-Tip up my nasal cavity. Any deeper and that stupid thing would've been tickling my brain. My eyes are instantly watering. Did she have to go so deep?

"There we go. All done. Give me about fifteen minutes and the doctor should be back in with the results, okay?"

"Okay. If it's not the flu, do you think I can go to ICU and see Ryker?"

"Sure, as long as your blood results don't come back with anything too crazy."

"I hope not. I need to see him."

She nods. "I'll see if I can get an update for you."

"Thank you. His daughter is out of town, and I'm the only person here for him right now. I don't want him to be alone."

"I understand. I'll keep you posted, and hopefully we can rule out the flu so you can actually go see him."

"I hope so."

Nurse Jessica leaves the room with my nasal probe in hand. A few seconds later June pops back into the room.

"My brother called and said he needed me to pick him up from work. Do you mind if I step out for a bit?"

"No, I plan on staying the night anyway."

V. Kelly

June smiles. "Gonna try to get daddy back, huh?"

"Ugh, please don't call him that. He's not my daddy."

"Right. Right. So, are you going to attempt to get *her* daddy back?" She lets out an unattractive snort, covering her mouth as she laughs at her own joke.

"I don't know. He hates me right now, but I need to know that he's okay. I don't expect him to take me back, but I don't want him to be alone right now either."

She nods in agreement. "You go, girl. Get you some of that big daddy cock."

"Will you please stop saying that?"

"Sure, but that takes away the fun of teasing you."

Thankfully, the doctor picks that moment to enter the room. He has a very concerned look on his face and sits in the rolling chair next to my bed.

"Amelia, I got back some of your test results. The good news is, you don't have the flu. The bad news is, well, maybe not so bad news. I guess it depends on how you take it . . ."

"Spit it out already, Doc," June yells.

The doctor looks a little taken aback, but chuckles. "Well, Amelia, your blood results came back and the reason you've been throwing up so much lately is because you're pregnant."

"Ha! I fucking knew it!" June shouts. "Bitch, I didn't even need to tell you to get some of that big daddy cock, you already claimed that shit and marked it as your own. If you lick it you stick it, right?" She puts up a fist expecting me to fist bump her, but I don't even lift my arm.

June's enthusiasm is not reciprocated.

How can I be pregnant? I've been on the pill the entire time I was living with Ryker. This has to be a mistake. I take my pills religiously. Same time every fucking day. There's no way I can be pregnant. No way at all.

Except . . .

Ah hell. While I was in the hospital and a few days after, I didn't take my birth control pills at all. I went almost a week without them. During that time Ryker and I did have sex.

This can't be happening.

But it totally is.

I'm pregnant.

I'm pregnant with Ryker's baby and he's . . .

Oh no!

I need to see Ryker as soon as possible. He can't die without knowing about his baby. He needs to live for us—for all three of us now.

Ryker

Warm embers of a smoldering flame flick and float in front of my eyes. Above me I see the fire burning bright, but down here I feel safe and sheltered from any harm. I lay my hands behind me and clutch the soft fabric of a flimsy bed sheet.

How the hell did I end up on a bed?

I sit up and stare around me. I'm in a black room with only a single window that is filled with a blinding white light. The floor is made of mirrored glass, and the ceiling is nothing but flames and fire.

"Hello," someone says to my left. The voice is tiny and a little high-pitched. I turn and see a small boy staring at me.

His vivid blue eyes shine brightly, dancing in tandem with the flames on the ceiling. He smiles—it's all teeth.

"Hello there," I reply, studying his impish little face.

The boy cocks his head to the side, like a lost puppy. The only expression on his face is a mix of sadness and pure joy.

"What are you doing here?" he asks me.

"I'm not sure. I don't know where *here* is. Who are you?"

"I don't know."

"How can you not know who you are?"

"Because I'm not supposed to be here."

"Where are your parents?" I ask him, searching the room for any kind of door. There's nothing, just the window, the boy, the fire, and me.

"What are parents?"

"You know, the people who raise and love you."

"Ohhhh, yeah, I don't have those."

"Why not? Are you lost?"

"No. I'm not supposed to be here," he answers as he carefully approaches me on the bed.

"Who are you?"

"My name is Ryker."

"Ohhhh," he says, jumping up beside me. He immediately begins kicking his legs since they can't touch the floor. He has to be around four or five.

"What's your name?" I ask him.

"I don't have one of those either."

"How is that possible?"

The flames above our heads crack and the boy flinches.

"They don't give us names where I come from."

"Where do you come from?"

He grins and points to my head. "There."

I'm instantly confused.

"What do you mean?"

"Well, I'm not really supposed to be here. You brought me here."

My face scrunches in confusion. "Where am I?"

The little boy jumps off the bed and takes my hand, leading me over to a window. The blinding white light forces me to close my eyes, it's way too intense to look at.

"Look," he instructs me.

I pry open one of my eyes and find myself looking into a hospital room. There are a few nurses standing over a bed and a doctor as well. Once they are finished doing whatever they are doing, they leave, and I see a man lying motionless on the bed.

That man is me.

"Am I dead?"

V. Kelly

"No," the boy answers.

"Am I alive?"

The boy nods. "Yes, but you could choose not to wake up."

"Why would I do that?" I question.

"Some people give up on life. They say it's too hard. I wouldn't know because I don't belong anywhere but here with you."

I glance at the boy to see what he's thinking, but his facial expression hasn't changed at all. He's still smiling and consumed with joy. How can anyone be joyful when they're stuck in limbo like this?

Staring at my practically dead body makes me uneasy. I back away from the window and sit back down on the small bed inside the room. The boy doesn't follow me.

"Who gave you your name?" He asks.

"My parents named me. Usually parents will name a child based on something they like or someone they know. My parents named me Ryker because they met on Rikers Island, it's a place in New York. They told me that once they found out that they were having a boy, there wasn't any other name they could picture him having. My dad didn't like the spelling of Rikers, so he changed it. He dropped the 'S' and added a 'Y' instead of the letter I."

The boy continues to stare out the window. "Maybe you can give me a name. You know, since I don't have parents to name me."

"You want me to give you a name?"

The boy looks over at me, still grinning like he's having the time of his life, even though his voice sounds depressed and a bit shaken.

"Yes. There's nobody else here to name me. Unless you have already named someone else."

"I have," I admit, my heart rate increases when I realize I may never get to hug my daughter again. "I have a daughter, her name is Haysleigh."

"Oh, Haysleigh does not sound like the right name for me. I like Ryker though. Can I have your name?"

The boy's innocence tugs on my heart strings. "Wouldn't you want a name of your own?"

"Well, you already named someone, and Ryker and Haysleigh are the only two names that I know. I should choose at least one of them."

"Technically, I didn't name Haysleigh. It's the name her mother chose for her."

It didn't seem possible, but the boy's smile actually gets bigger. "Does that mean you can give me a name?"

"I guess so, but I have no idea what to call you."

"What would you name Haysleigh if she had been a boy?"

I ponder his question for quite a long time. Haysleigh's mother didn't give me the chance to name her. She had already chosen her name before she was even born. I had this book of names my mother gave me when she found out she was going to be a grandma, and I remember circling a few that I liked. One name stood out more than any of the others.

"Jonah," I whisper. "If Haysleigh had been a boy, I would've named her Jonah.

The little boy jumps high into the air and screams. "I loooove it! Jonah, that's gonna be my name."

I watch the boy dance and skip around me, his smile warming every bone deep inside. His smile is infectious and soon my own lips are sliding into a grin.

V. Kelly

He rushes over to me and gives me a strong hug. His tiny arms grip my waist the best they can. "Thank you, Ryker. Thank you so much for giving me a name. People don't know what it's like to walk around in the nothing without a name. I probably should go now. I'm not supposed to be here."

"Jonah, wait. I don't want to be here alone."

"You're not alone, Ryker. She's been here the whole time?" he states, motioning to the window.

"Who has?"

"See for yourself."

I get up from the bed and walk over to the window. I'm still lying in the bed, not moving, but this time I'm not surrounded by doctors. Someone is holding my hand, crying into my palm with her salty tears.

Amelia.

"She's been here every day. She looks sad. You should probably wake up and talk to her."

"I'm angry with her," I whisper, wiping away the single tear that's slithering down my face like a sneaky serpent. "She betrayed me."

Amelia looks absolutely devastated.

I can't hear a word that she's saying, but from her body language alone, I can tell she's asking me to stay and not leave her. Her lips touch down on my hand and I see them tell me over and over again how sorry she is and that she loves me.

"I love you, too," I scream through the glass.

"Anger and betrayal often walk hand in hand. Those are the kind of emotions that can eat away a person's soul. That's why I never let myself feel anything but happy. Happiness and love are all a person needs to survive. Once you let go of that anger inside of you, your body will seek out the joy it needs to continue on.

Don't be like the others and give up because something in your life didn't go the way you wanted it to. Fight for love. Fight for her. She needs you just as much as you need her."

I stare at the young boy in complete awe. How can so much wisdom come out of someone that tiny?

I feel him tug my hand. "Jonah must leave now, Ryker. I can't decide what happens next for you. Just know, that no matter what you choose, Jonah will always be right here with you." He pats my chest right above my heart. "A little joy to follow you around wherever you will go. Goodbye, Ryker."

"Goodbye, Jonah."

I watch him dissolve into tiny little embers that float up towards the ceiling and disappear into the flames above my head.

Watching him go makes me feel even more alone.

To my left I hear a large rumbling sound as the wall tears apart and reveals a doorway leading out of the room.

I stand there for a few seconds wondering where the door will lead and if I should go through it. I almost decide to stay where I am until I hear the soft whisper of a sobbing voice begging me to move forward. It's Amelia.

"Ryker, please come back to me," she cries.

Hearing her voice is the only motivation that I need. I take one cautious step forward, then I run.

Amelia

I leave the emergency room in a daze. Half living, half dead inside. My thoughts keep circling back to the tiny life blossoming in my womb. It's a piece of me and Ryker. It should be a beautiful blessing, but all I can think about is the hurt in Ryker's eyes after he heard what I said, and the void in my heart that I feel without him. Raising this baby without Ryker is something I don't want to imagine. He's everything to me, and I wish I knew how to explain that without sounding like an ass.

June tries to comfort me the best she can, but I'm on a mission to see Ryker, and no one is going to stop me.

"May I help you?" The receptionist asks when I approach her desk.

"Ryker Thompson is in the ICU, I'd like to see him, please."

"ICU patients can't have visitors. Let me check what his status is, and we can go from there." The woman looks to be in her sixties, with silver-gray hair done up in a bun. I notice she has three pencils sticking out of her top knot, one is the typical yellow pencil, but the other two are decorated with lady bugs and butterflies. She pushes her glasses up her nose and brings her face incredibly close to the screen.

"They just moved him out of ICU. His condition must have stabilized."

"Can I see him?"

"Are you family?"

I want to tell her I'm his daughter, but the little gem inside my tummy makes me think twice about it.

"No. I'm a family friend."

"I'm sorry, but where he's located only family can visit."

I'm hit with a sudden wave of nausea, panic, and complete despair. "You don't understand. I need to see him."

"I'm sorry, but only family can visit him at this time."

I slam both of my hands onto her desk, anger flashing in my eyes. "Listen here, Lady, I've been through hell and back these past few weeks, and the only person that gives a shit about me might be dying behind those doors. Right now, I'm the only person who cares about him. His own daughter doesn't want to drop whatever she's doing to be here and doesn't seem to give a shit that he's in the hospital. Someone needs to be here for him right now, and that person is me. I don't care who you need to talk to in order to make this happen, but I'm not leaving until I can see him." I'm shouting so loud the rest of the people in the lobby are staring at me like I'm fucking Medusa.

"You better listen to her, Ruth, this chick's hormonal."

I glare at June, but don't correct her because she's right, I am hormonal.

"I'm sorry, but my hands are tied." Ruth doesn't seem to give a shit about my emotions or that I'm on the verge of breaking down into a puddle of tears if she doesn't let me see Ryker. She also doesn't care that her bright eggplant-colored scarf doesn't match her neon green top, either, but you don't see me making a snide comment about it, even though I want to.

"What's going on?" Nurse Jessica asks when she suddenly appears behind the receptionist.

"I've politely informed this woman that only family members can see patients just out of ICU. She's not listening to me,"

V. Kelly

Ruth's tone is flat and riddled with annoyance. She can continue being annoyed all she wants; it's not going to change my mission.

"Ruth, I can personally vouch for this woman. The man she is trying to see basically raised her since she was six years old. He's not her biological father, but he's like a father to her, and they have a very *special* relationship. She was in the hospital a few weeks back and he was here every day with her. Please give her a visitor's pass, I will personally take responsibility for her." Jessica emphasizes the word special like she secretly knows what's going on between me and Ryker, but that's impossible. We weren't even a thing back when we first met her.

Ruth sighs. "Fine, as long as it's not my neck on the line. I don't care what she does. I have two more years before I can retire and then be done with people like her."

"She's pregnant," Jessica states as if that will make a difference, "she just found out, so please forgive her hormonal outburst."

Ruth rolls her eyes and hands me a visitor's pass before she shoos me away from her desk.

"I'm going to go get my brother, Mia. If you need me to pick you up later, call me," June says right before she gives me a quick hug and runs off.

"Thank you for being here for me, June."

"What are friends for?" she asks as she bolts out the front door. In my head I can't help thinking about Haysleigh, who, before June, had always been there for me. A part of me wishes she had never betrayed my trust; the other part of me still can't stand looking at her face. I must admit, I do miss her, but I also don't know if I can ever forget what happened between us or what she did to me. After the blow up at her dad's house, she probably feels the same way.

"Come on, Amelia, follow me. I'll take you to see him."

"Thank you," I tell Jessica as she leads me away from the receptionist's desk. "You didn't have to do this for me, but I'm really glad you did."

"Hey, if I was carrying someone's baby and they were hurt, I'd want to see them, too. Just because you aren't married or engaged or even related, doesn't mean you shouldn't be able to see him."

"Wait, how did you know that it was his baby?"

"I didn't. I had a hunch that the baby might be his because of the way he was looking at you in the hospital. Also, because he defended your honor when your ex popped in on you unexpectedly. Men don't just assault someone like that without underlying feelings being involved."

I frown. "I've messed up so much shit lately that I'm surprised anyone has any feeling for me other than loathing hate."

Jessica puts a friendly hand on my shoulder. "Sometimes in life we make monumental mistakes that seem too big for us to overcome. It's the steps that we take to overcome those mistakes that make us human. The best part about living is that the past always stays behind us. You can always take a step forward to move on, but you can never take a step back to change the past. That's why they say love can move mountains. A mistake is nothing more than a ginormous mountain that you need to climb. If someone truly loves you, they will see past what you have done to them and forgive you regardless of how much you've hurt them."

"You're pretty wise for a nurse."

V. Kelly

"You learn a lot working with people every day. My older patients have given me some great advice over the years, and I've absorbed it." We stop in front of a room marked 1A. "Ryker's behind this door. I'm rooting for you two to work things out. I see love every day in these halls, but when I look at you two, I see more than love. I see your souls intertwined in perfect harmony. You might not think you fit together, but sometimes God has other plans for us. Love shouldn't be defined by age gaps and what other people consider normal. All that matters, is what's in here," she says patting my heart, "and now here." She gentle touches my stomach.

"Thanks, Jessica. I'm sorry I wanted to gouge out your eyeballs when we first met."

Her eyes round.

"You were looking at Ryker and undressing him with your eyes and stuff. The little green-eyed monster kinda took over me that day. Plus, I just survived almost dying in a fire."

Nurse Jessica smiles, "I guess I'll let it slide, but remind me to keep the scalpels away from you while you're here."

I chuckle, "Yeah, probably a good idea. I was just kidding by the way; I would never actually gouge out your eyeballs. Thanks again for getting me back here. Now I have to do the hard part and make him forgive me."

"If he really loves you, he will. Take care of yourself, Amelia."

"I'll try."

She opens the door for me and my heart stops when I see Ryker lying in the bed. He's extremely pale except for a few black smudges around his hair line. He has bandages up and down his arms and legs, and he's hooked up to a bunch of machines.

I rush over to his side and drop down next to him, carefully taking his hand in mine.

"Ryker, I'm sorry." I kiss the back of his hand, tears already forming in my eyes.

His eyes are closed. I barely hear his breath over the heart monitor beeps and the sound of the IV machine dropping saline into his body through the cords.

Why did this have to happen?

How did he get hurt?

Ryker has always been so careful when he's working.

Did our fight distract him?

Am I responsible for this?

I try to shake the thoughts out of my head, but I can't.

"Please, don't die," I beg him, squeezing his hand even tighter. It's wrapped in gauze, but there is a small space where his fingers are sticking out and I brush the skin on his hand, desperate to connect with him physically again.

"You know, I didn't know what to say to you whenever I saw you again. Apologizing doesn't feel like enough. Begging seemed like too much. I've been miserable since I left you. I can't eat. I can't sleep. I've been sick as hell. I know it's because I love you, Ryker. It sounds stupid, but I need you. You're the only person in this world that matters to me and has always been there for me."

I start to cry, using the bandage around his hand to wipe up my tears.

"Please don't die."

V. Kelly

I sit next to his bed for the next two days, watching his chest slowly rise and fall, nothing changing other than slow beep of his heart rate monitor.

I spend most of my day just holding his hand, falling asleep draped over the side of his hospital bed, waiting for him to wake up. June stopped in a few times and brought me food and a change of clothes. I've refused to leave Ryker's side. Haysleigh still hasn't shown up at the hospital. I wonder what's so important in Vegas that she can't be bothered by her dad? I send her messages about his progress and what the doctors tell me, but she only hits that stupid thumbs up button and never really responds.

I wish he would wake up.

It's almost noon and I've not let go of Ryker's hand since I woke up this morning. I give his hand a light little squeeze and kiss it, like I've done a million times since he got here.

This time, I feel his fingers slightly twitch in response.

I look up.

Ryker's eyes are open, but he's staring at me strangely.

"Amelia?" he chokes out.

"Ryker!" I squeak. "You're alive!"

I can't stop my tears. They are falling swiftly down my face. Each one is another vulnerable part of me that I need to release.

"What happened?"

"You were hurt in a fire. You were in ICU for a couple hours, but the doctor's say that you're better now."

"Everything hurts," he groans. He's quiet for a second before he speaks again. "Why are you here?" he questions.

Why am I here? Well, let's see . . . I love you. I'm pregnant with your baby, and I'm fucking sorry. Yup, that's exactly why I'm here.

"I didn't want you to be alone," I whisper.

"Oh," he replies weakly.

"Oh," I repeat.

"Ryker, I'm so sorry. I messed everything up. I've waited my whole life for you to love me, and then I go and say the stupidest thing ever, making a mockery of this beautiful thing we have with each other. It was the worst mistake I've ever made, and I know you will never forgive me, but I need you to know that what I felt for you was real—all of it. I'm in love with you, and I don't think there's anything that will ever stop me from loving you." I squeeze his hand, desperate for some indication that he feels the same way, but he just stares at me, saying nothing.

The doctor comes in a few minutes later and kindly asks me to leave the room. I contemplate leaving altogether, but I'm determined to make Ryker talk to me—even if he doesn't want to.

Ryker

I don't have it in my heart to ask Amelia to leave. I've been here six days and she hasn't left my side. I let her hold my hand because it's comforting, but I don't talk to her.

It's a little childish of me, but I don't know what to say. She's tried to apologize to me a few times, but each time I blow her off.

It still hurts—everything hurts.

The doctor says I broke three of my ribs in the fall. I have second-degree burns on my arms and legs, and a broken tibia in my left leg. I'm probably going to need physical therapy, but for right now, the only thing that helps my pain is lying flat on the bed, and the occasional squeeze of Amelia's comforting hand.

Haysleigh hasn't shown up at all. Amelia said that she was in Vegas and I'm hoping she didn't do something stupid just to spite me. If she did, I guess I'll have to accept it and kill Willis when he gets back.

Amelia gets up to leave the room to go get something from the cafeteria. I don't say anything to her when she leaves, but my eyes trail after her wishing she would stay.

It's hard to ignore her.

I love her. There's no doubt about that in my mind, but after what happened with Haysleigh, a relationship will never work out between us. Haysleigh made sure of that.

I'm about to fall asleep when I hear someone shuffle into the room, I'm expecting it to be Amelia, but I see Haysleigh standing by my bed instead.

"Hey," she whispers.

I can already tell she's getting emotional. Her bottom lip is quivering, and tears are filling up her big brown eyes.

"Hey," I whisper back.

"How are you feeling?"

"Like I fell through two floors of a building." I shift uncomfortably and try to adjust the bed so I can look her in the eye.

"Daddy, I'm so sorry."

"It's okay."

"No, it's not. I said some petty shit to you and Mia. I was shocked when I walked in on you two fucking and I didn't know how to feel in that moment. I'm sorry if I hurt you."

She takes my hand and I notice she's not wearing her engagement ring anymore.

"Where's Willis?"

"In Vegas. We went down there to elope, but I walked in on him fucking a stripper during his bachelor party and broke up with him. I guess I dodged a pretty big bullet."

"Yes, you did."

"Do you forgive me?"

"I want to, Haysleigh, but it's hard. I saw a side of you that night that I'm not proud of. What you did to Amelia was cruel. She didn't deserve any of that."

"I know," she whimpers. Tears start dripping from her eyes. I squeeze her hand to comfort her.

"I can't believe I let him fuck me like a dog. I ruined my only friendship for a stupid unfaithful guy."

"Yes, you did."

"Do you hate me?"

I sigh, "I could never hate you, Haysleigh. I don't hate anyone. I don't even hate your mother for what she did to us."

Thinking about Courtney after all these years is hard. When Haysleigh was six months old, she tried to give her up for adoption. She didn't even tell me about it. When I found out, I immediately went and filed for full custody of Haysleigh. There was no way I was going to allow Courtney to give Haysleigh away. Courtney said she wasn't ready to be a mom, but I was ready to be a dad the moment I held Haysleigh in my arms. I knew I would do anything for her that day. It didn't matter that I was only sixteen and didn't have any way to support her. I was determined to find a way. Haysleigh was the most precious thing in my life, and I was going to protect her at all costs.

Courtney signed over all her parental rights to me before she disappeared. She never spoke to me or Haysleigh ever again. We occasionally received a birthday card in the mail. It would come with no return address so Haysleigh could never write her back, but she always signed it with a C. She didn't write anything special in the cards. It would say something generic, like *I hope you have the best birthday ever*, but it meant a lot to Haysleigh that her mom would write her sometimes. It meant something to me, too, but I was glad she stayed away. Courtney wasn't fit to be a mother, and there's no telling what would've happened to Haysleigh if she had stayed in her life.

"Do you hate Amelia?" she asks.

I shake my head. "I can't hate her."

"Because you love her."

I nod. "I just can't look at her the same anymore."

"For what it's worth I think she really loves you, Dad." She squeezes my hand. "I think it's beyond weird, but I've never seen her this miserable. She wasn't even this depressed over me and Willis fucking behind her back."

"You saw her?"

"She's in the hallway. We talked before I came in here."

I wonder why Amelia hasn't come back in. She hasn't left my side since I got brought out of ICU.

"I think you should talk to her."

Her comment catches me completely off guard. I did not expect her to say that. "What?" I question, not completely sure I heard her right. "Why?"

"Because you love each other, Dad. Love is important if it's real. I think I always knew you guys had feelings for each other, but I tried to block my suspicions out because it was way too weird for me. We both almost lost you, and I realize that life is too short to hold stupid grudges. If you love her, you should forgive her. That's what people do when they really care about someone."

I well up, tears pricking my eyes like tiny thorns. It almost sounds like Haysleigh is giving me her blessing to date Amelia, but that can't be possible. There's no way this is real.

"Why are you saying all this?"

"Because it's the right thing to do. You deserve to be happy, Dad. If Mia makes you happy, then you should pursue the relationship, even if it makes me feel all icky and gross."

I laugh.

"I'm serious, Dad. Who am I to stand in the way of true love? What Willis and I had felt amazing, but it wasn't real. What you and Amelia have is deeper than that. It's almost cosmic in a way."

V. Kelly

She has a point. There are times when I feel like the stars were aligned just so Amelia and I can be together.

"I don't know. I don't want to make you uncomfortable, and I definitely don't want you to fight with her anymore."

"I won't. I'm over that now. I might be a little uncomfortable at first, but I'll get over it. But I swear, if you expect me to call her mommy, that's where I draw the line. She's definitely not my fucking mommy."

We both laugh. She bends down and gives me a tight hug. It hurts, but I push the pain out of my head so I can enjoy connecting with my daughter again. I missed holding her like this.

"Daddy, I'm so sorry I didn't come earlier. I love you. I don't know what I would've done if I had lost you."

"It's okay. I love you, too. I'm alive and still here, that's all that matters."

She nods her head in agreement. "I'm glad you're alive, Old Man. Life would be boring without you."

"Likewise, Kiddo."

Haysleigh gives me one last hug before she starts to leave the room.

"Hey, Haysleigh," I call after her.

"Yeah?"

"Thank you," I tell her.

"Always." She walks out the door just as Amelia starts walking in. They give each other a sympathetic look, exchange a few quiet words that I can't exactly hear, and then keep walking in opposite directions.

"Hey," Amelia says, settling by the bed. She grabs my hand and gives it a loving squeeze.

My head starts swirling with all sorts of crazy thoughts as I look into her eyes. I could probably continue playing the silent game with her, but that's not getting us anywhere. I miss her—I miss her like crazy. Staying quiet isn't going to fix what happened between us, but what I say next might.

"Hey," I whisper.

It takes every ounce of strength I have to change my frown into a smile, but I do it, because I need to. It's time to let her back in.

Amelia

"Well, well, look what the whore dragged in," Haysleigh's annoying voice invades my thoughts.

I don't even bother looking up at her. I've got more important things to worry about than her being a bitch to me.

I'm sitting on a bench a few doors down from Ryker's door. I've been trying to figure out a way to tell Ryker about the baby, but he's not talking to me and I feel like I deserve his silence.

It's the first time she's been to the hospital since her dad got here. I'm too weak to confront her about it. The last thing I need right now is another cat fight.

Haysleigh starts to walk past me but stops a few feet away.

"What's wrong?" she questions.

"Nothing," I mumble.

"Mia, I've known you since you were six. I know when you're having a mini meltdown. Spill the tea. What's got you all upset? Is it about my dad?

I nod.

"Is he okay?

I nod again.

"Mia, talk to me. I know we aren't speaking right now, and I said some pretty fucked up shit at my dad's house, but I still care if you're okay. Please tell me what's wrong."

I stare at my stomach and grimace.

"What's wrong?" she prods again.

"I'm pregnant," I whisper. Saying the words out loud is scary. When I was holding it in, I could pretend that everything was normal, but now everything is out in the open and I can't take back my words even if I tried.

"Is it my dad's?"

I burst into tears, weakly nodding my head.

"Does he know?"

I shake my head in response.

Talking is ridiculously hard right now. I can see why Ryker's not doing it.

Haysleigh plops into the chair beside me and leans her head against the wall.

"This is some fucked up shit, Mia. My dad's hurt, we hate each other, and now you're telling me that you're carrying around my brother or sister inside of you? This feels like a fucked-up episode of *Jerry Springer*.

I force myself to look up at her.

"I didn't mean for any of this to happen, Haysleigh. I went into this with the intent to hurt you but ended up hurting myself instead. I have strong feelings for your dad. Maybe I always have, because I fell in love with him so easily. I never meant to hurt either one of you. Everything is so fucked up and if I lose your dad, I've lost everything I care about. I already lost you, I can't lose him, too."

She gently takes my hand.

"Look, I may think you're a pretty sick person for fucking my dad, but after what I did, I can't hold it against you. I think I've always known that you liked him, but it wasn't until I saw you here, sitting on this bench looking like a disheveled mess, that I realized how much you really love him. All I want is for you both to be happy. If that means I have to watch you guys be together, which is major yuck by the way, so be it. Who am I to stand in the way of true love?"

"Do you really mean that?"

"After the week I've had, I've realized that life's too short to hold grudges over petty shit anymore. So yes, I mean it. I just want you both to be happy."

"What about Willis?"

She chuckles. "That guy is a dick. We went to Vegas to elope and I found him the night before our wedding fucking some stripper in our hotel room. I broke shit off with him." She shows me her hand. "See, no ring. I've spent the last week trying to get home. It cost too much to change my flight plans, so I had to wait until my flight was scheduled to come home."

"I'm sorry," I reply. I really mean it, too. I'm sorry that Willis hurt Haysleigh like he hurt me, and that she couldn't get home to see her dad. But I'm also thankful things didn't work out between them. That would've been beyond awkward.

"Don't worry about it. Karma's a bitch, and it came back to bite me in my ass. I'm just glad I figured it out before I became Mrs. Willis Dickwell."

I laugh. I never gave much thought about what my last name would've been if I married Willis, but hearing it out loud, I'm glad I dodged the Dickwell bullet, too.

"I'm sorry for what I said to you, Mia. I don't really think that you're pathetic or that you should disappear. I was just shocked to find you riding my dad's cock like a horse jockey."

I grimace, realizing that if I found my dad dick deep in Haysleigh, I probably would've acted the same way.

"I'm sorry for what I said to you, Haysleigh. I was angry and upset, and some things you said really hurt me, but I'm not gonna lie, I miss you."

"I miss you, too." She grabs my hand and squeezes it. "How about we call a truce and work our way back up to being friends again? We both did some pretty crazy things, but I don't want our friendship to end, Mia. I still consider you my best friend."

"I still consider you my best friend, too. I like the sound of a truce. This past month has tortured me."

"Me, too. Hey, I'm gonna go say hi to my dad. Can you wait out here for a few minutes? I need to apologize to him, but I want to do it in private."

"Sure."

She starts to get up.

"Haysleigh?"

"Yeah?"

"Thanks, for being here for me. I know my situation is really fucked up, but for what it's worth, I hope you know that I really do love your dad."

"I know that now, Mia. I'll be back in a few."

I watch her walk down the hall. As she walks away, I feel little pieces of the ice surrounding my heart start to chisel away. It feels good to get rid of some of this excess emotional baggage fighting with Haysleigh has created inside of me.

I'm slowly working on feeling better.

Talking to Haysleigh was a baby step I needed to take in order to repair myself. Now all I need to do is convince Ryker to forgive me, too.

I hover outside Ryker's door, wondering if I should go inside. His silent treatment has been absolute torture the last few days.

V. Kelly

At least he's looking at me now, that's something he wasn't doing before.

Haysleigh comes out of the room and pats me on the shoulder as I begin to walk in. "He's all yours." She starts to walk away. "Mia?"

"Yeah?"

"Take care of my dad, okay?"

"I will."

"Is it okay if I call you later?"

"Sure."

"Thanks." Haysleigh's lips lift into a smile, before she shoves her hands into her pockets and begins walking down the hall.

I take a deep breath. *Here goes nothing.*

Ryker watches me walk in. I can't tell if he's happy to see me or sad. There are tears in his eyes that weren't there when I left.

I walk over to the chair beside his bed and sit in it. "Hey," I tell him, giving his hand a squeeze.

He squeezes my hand back but doesn't say anything at first. He continues staring at me. I hang my head, wishing he would say something to open the lines of communication between us.

After a few minutes of awkward silence, he shifts on the bed and says, "Hey."

My head shoots up. He's still staring at me strangely. Maybe I imagined him talking to me because I'm desperate to hear his voice.

"Did you just talk?"

He laughs. "Yeah, I'm sorry I've been giving you the silent treatment. It was childish of me. It was easier to not say anything than to confront what happened between us."

His fingers gently play with the palm of my hand.

"I'm sorry, Ryker." A few stray tears glide down my face, but I'm too weak to brush them away. "I know I've said this before, but I really am sorry. What I said to Haysleigh was wrong on so many levels. I was angry and upset and things that I had been thinking and feeling came bubbling up like an underground well."

He nods. "I understand. It doesn't make what you said okay, but it helps me understand a little more."

I decide it's time to come clean. If Ryker and I are meant to be together, he's going to have to know everything. All the fucked-up details that brought us together—even if it destroys all my chances of being with him.

"I need to tell you something. I . . . I started the fire on purpose. I mean, I wanted to set Willis' stuff on fire already, but I was hoping the fire would get big enough that you would show up to save me. It was really messed up. I never meant for my whole house to catch on fire, but I did want you to come. I had this stupid thought in my head that if I could seduce you and get you to fall for me, then I could get back at Haysleigh."

I watch his small smile turn into a scowl. He's about to say something, but I hold up my hand to silence him.

"I'm not finished. Let me say everything I need to say and then you can go off on me."

He frowns.

"I initially did want to use you for revenge, but then you saved my life, you opened your home to me, you showed me what it was like to be loved unconditionally by another person, and you were there for me when no one else was. After that, revenge didn't matter to me anymore. All that mattered was being with you. I fell for you hard, Ryker. It was so easy to fall in love with you because I've always been in love with you. This whole thing

V. Kelly

may have started out as my way of getting revenge on Haysleigh, but what came out of it means more to me than revenge ever would. I love you. I don't care if you end up hating me for the rest of my life. It won't change my feelings for you." My emotions are going so crazy that I can't keep up with my tears. All I want is for Ryker to forgive me—I need him to forgive me.

Ryker's eyes are shimmering, a single tear runs down his cheek, he quickly swipes it away.

"I love you, too. I always have. What you said that night really hurt me, but I thank you for being honest with me, Amelia. I know that must've been difficult for you."

"It really was."

He breathes out loudly, groaning as he tries to sit up in the bed.

"Listen. I know we can't take back what happened, but these past few weeks have been awful. The house feels empty without you and Slinky in it. I thought it would be easier staying away from you than it would be to try to work things out. I thought Haysleigh would hate us both after what happened, but after the talk I just had with her, I think we'll be okay. If you're open to trying again, so am I."

My heart feels like a baby bird that just learned to fly. Ryker wants to try again! He wants to be with me. Every thought that pops into my head is like happy little bubbles floating on the breeze. I'm content in that happy place until I realize the secret I've been holding in—a secret that I'm going to have to tell him before we can go any further.

My face falls. My hand begins trembling and I can barely hold on to his hand anymore.

How will he take the news?

Will he still want to be with me if he finds out?

"Amelia? What's wrong?"

The tears falling from my eyes turn into rushing waterfalls. My chest seizes up in a choking sob as I try to figure out how to tell him about the baby without making him run away.

"Amelia, baby, what's wrong."

I barely get through the words, but somehow, I manage to find my voice. Dreading each and every word that I'm about to say.

"I need to tell you something, and I hope it doesn't change anything you just said."

"You're scaring me," he remarks, his voice cautious and concerned.

"I . . . I don't know how this happened. I mean, I do, but I still never meant for this to happen, Ryker. Please don't hate me."

"Amelia, what the hell is going on?"

"I'm pregnant," I manage to choke out. "I didn't mean to get pregnant, but I did. It's your baby. I'm pregnant with your baby, Ryker. Please don't make me give the baby up for adoption or have an abortion. I know it's my fault that I got pregnant, but I don't think I can get rid of the baby. It's a part of us."

His eyes widen.

Is that surprise or fear in his eyes? I try to read his facial expression, but it's like he's wearing a mask. I start bawling again, this time dropping my head onto the bed so I can cry into my arms. I feel his hand move up my arm and slowly start moving through my hair.

"Hey now, I would never ask you to do that. I know I said that I wasn't ready to have another kid, but I also said we would make it work if it ever happened. This is my fault, too. I didn't use a condom. You can't take all the blame for this. This baby is a part of us, and there's no way I'd want to give either of you up."

V. Kelly

My head shoots up, I can barely see his smiling face through my tears. "Do you really mean that?"

"Of course, I do. I love you, Amelia, and I love our baby, too. I don't even have to meet them to know that. This baby was made from our love. Sure, that love came in fast like a tornado, and we both got caught up in the turmoil that swirled around us, but even tornados have a center of peace inside of them. That's where we found each other, Amelia—deep in the heart of the tornado. It doesn't matter if that storm was meant to destroy us, we both survived the aftermath. We have a lot of debris to clean up, but that's common after a storm as reckless as ours."

His analogy makes me fall for him even harder. This man—a man so much older and wiser than me, knows exactly what to say to make everything better. It's why I fell in love with him. I can't picture myself with anyone else now—only Ryker.

"You have no idea how relieved I am to hear you say that. I totally thought you were going to throw me out of your room and tell me to leave."

His face softens. "Never. You're stuck with me, Amelia. From this day forward, we're going to do this together, okay?"

"Okay."

"I do have a request though before we go any further. If you don't mind."

"Of course! I'd do anything for you, Ryker. Whatever it is, just ask."

He clears his throat and looks slightly uncomfortable. "This is going to sound completely weird, and you're probably going to think I'm crazy, but if our baby is a boy, do you mind if we name him Jonah?"

Inside of my chest, I can feel my heart already melting. He wants to name our baby! That means he really wants to be with me.

"Oh my gosh, I absolutely love that name. Yes! We can definitely name the baby Jonah if it's a boy."

A look of relief washes over Ryker's face. "Thank goodness. If you hated that name, it would kill me."

"No, I love it. Almost as much as I love you." I kiss the back of his hand, and then gently place my hand over my stomach. "You hear that little guy, if you're a boy your name's going to be Jonah." I look up at Ryker who's smiling so widely I'm surprised his smile isn't touching his ears.

"Amelia," he whispers.

"Yes?"

"I have one more question for you."

"Okay?"

"I can't exactly get down on one knee and ask you this properly, but would you make me the happiest man in the world and marry me? There's nothing I want more in this world than making you my wife."

Yup, more tears. I can't seem to stop them.

This time I jump out of the chair I'm sitting in and fling myself over the top of him. He groans in protest because I accidentally hit one of his broken ribs on impact, but he doesn't ask me to get off him, instead he grabs my chin and directs my eyes so I can look at him.

"Is that a yes?"

"No," I pause. "That's a hell fucking yes.

He chuckles before drawing me in for a much-needed kiss. His lips are comforting. I soak them in, scratching into my memory the softness of his pout and the tenderness of his caresses. I never want to forget what they feel like. Three weeks was way too long to be without him. I can't spend another minute without this man in my life. Now that we sort of have Haysleigh's blessing, it seems like we can finally be together without having to worry about the consequences.

It sucks that it took starting a fire to bring us together, but it's because the flames of our love burn so bright that we keep going. Maybe that's what love truly is . . . one massive ball of flames struggling to survive. That's why I know that Ryker and I will make it.

From the beginning, our love was like a forest fire. It burned hot and wild from the moment we fell for each other. It was unpredictable at times and nearly destroyed us both. There were times where it seemed totally out of control and there was no hope of containing it, but like a smoldering piece of ember floating in the breeze, we survived. We rode the wind as it carried us apart, only to come together again reigniting the flames that attracted us both. We've become stronger because of it, and I know that whatever obstacles try to stand in our way, we'll smash through them together.

Because a love like ours doesn't die.

It burns.

Epilogue

Ryker

It's been almost five years since the day I almost died in that fire. Since then, my life has been a whirlwind of wonderful blessings I thank God every day for.

About a year after I asked Amelia to marry me, we ended up tying the knot at the local courthouse. Neither of us wanted a big wedding. All that mattered at the time was being together. She looked so beautiful in her dress. It was an off-white chiffon with a dangerous plunging neckline, much like the silver dress that got us into so much trouble when Haysleigh found out about our relationship.

Haysleigh is a lot better now. I think she accepts my relationship with Amelia, even though it makes her uncomfortable. Having Jonah has helped her be more receptive. She absolutely adores her little brother and has taken on the big sister role like a champ.

She even held Jonah for us while Amelia and I said our vows. It was nice to share that moment with her. I'm glad she was there to support us, even though she's still apprehensive about the relationship.

Amelia has been the perfect mommy and wife. Every day, I thank God that he spared me that night of the fire. If I hadn't survived, I would've never known what it was like to look into

V. Kelly

Amelia's eyes as I put a wedding ring around her finger or held Jonah in my arms.

I'd like to say that he looks like the boy from my dream, but he doesn't. Jonah looks exactly like his momma, same bright blue eyes and wild blonde hair that's not easy to tame. He's got more of my personality than hers. He's spunky, bright, and also loves playing with fire trucks just like his daddy. Overall, he keeps me pretty busy. Jonah is a bundle of energy that this old man has a hard time keeping up with. He's definitely his own unique person. Though he does share one thing in common with the Jonah I met while in limbo . . . they both have nothing but joy in their eyes.

That's one of the many things I love about him—Jonah is always happy.

Today he looks even more joyful than usual. He loves dressing up and his momma bought him a cute little tuxedo to wear for today's festivities.

"You ready?" I ask Haysleigh, taking her hand.

This is only the second time in my life that a woman has taken my breath away while wearing a wedding dress. The first time was when I married Amelia, now it's while I stare into Haysleigh's nervous eyes. She looks absolutely stunning today in her floor-length gown with an empire waist. Her long brown hair hangs over her shoulders and she has a small amount of baby's breath near the barrette that's holding some of her hair back.

It's hard to keep my emotions contained because the little girl I raised is no longer a little girl anymore. She's a woman—a very beautiful woman that I'm about to give away.

I've dreaded this day since she was born. Giving away their baby girl is something no father wants to do, but here I am, standing behind the closed doors of the church, ready to give away the most beautiful daughter any guy could ask for.

I actually approve of the man she's marrying. His name is Sonny, and he's the son of Amelia's old boss, Bodhi. Amelia introduced them one day when Haysleigh popped in for a lunch date with her.

They've been together for almost three years, and I have to admit, I like him. The man actually showed up on my doorstep, without her by his side, to ask me for her hand in marriage. Unlike that stupid shit Willis who broke both of my girl's hearts, Sonny actually has a backbone. When he shook my hand and asked me for Haysleigh's hand in marriage, I sat him down and had a very long talk with him. It didn't take me long to realize that the guy was legit and was head over heels in love with my daughter.

If I'm going to be totally honest, he had my blessing the second he knocked on my door. I have a lot of respect for any man that can look a father in his eye and ask for his blessing to marry his daughter.

Haysleigh is looking up at me with tears in her eyes. I can't tell if they are nervous tears or if she's upset. I'm doing my best to hold my own tears back, but it's hard. This dad's heart started melting the second she walked through that door in her beautiful wedding dress.

"I bet she didn't come," Haysleigh cries, flinging herself into my arms.

My heart instantly breaks for her. Those aren't nervous tears at all, they're sad tears—tears she shouldn't be having on her wedding day.

I don't like seeing Haysleigh upset like this. I tapped all my resources to track down Courtney before the wedding. All

V. Kelly

Haysleigh wanted today was for her mother to show up and see her get married. I wish I could say that Courtney was happy to hear from us, but she never responded to my letter, nor did she answer the phone when I called. Just once, I'd like Courtney to pretend she cares about her daughter.

"Even if she didn't, that doesn't mean she doesn't love you, Haysleigh. It means she doesn't realize what she's missing out on."

She sniffs. "All I wanted was for her to be there for me just this once. It's not like she's been here for anything else in my life."

I pull Haysleigh into my arms and hug her tightly. I know she's breaking apart inside, but there's nothing I can do to fix the damage twenty-six years without a mother has done to her. All I can do is let her know that I'm here for her no matter what.

"Hey now, don't cry." I wipe some tears away from her face. "It's your wedding day. When you walk through that door, you're going to have a man standing by that altar waiting for you. He's going to be looking at you with nothing but love in his eyes. That kind of love is all you need right now, Haysleigh. I know that your mom not showing up today is really hard on you, but you have to look at the positive things in your life. You will always have me, Amelia, and your brother standing beside you. Now you will have Sonny to lean on as well."

She smiles. "I know, Dad. Having you in my corner for all these years has meant the world to me. I'm so glad you love Sonny as much as I do. Your approval is everything."

"Well, I wouldn't say I love him," I kid.

She punches me playfully on the arm.

"You wouldn't be giving me away if you didn't, Old Man."

"Very true, Kiddo. Okay, it's time to dry up these tears. Everyone's waiting for your big arrival. They can't start this wedding without you.

She inhales deeply. "I'm ready."

I nod to the ushers standing by the doors and link arms with Haysleigh as they open the church doors for us.

The *Wedding March* begins to play, as we start our slow march towards the altar.

I briefly glance over at Haysleigh. My heart swells when I notice her beautiful face start to blush the second she sees that her groom is crying. Sonny is standing next to the priest. His long hippie hair is tied up into a man-bun today, but he's given up his normal hemp clothing for a more traditional tuxedo. The moment he sees Haysleigh, he's wiping away the tears on his face with the back of his hand.

These two kids really do love each other.

Amelia is standing across from Sonny holding a bouquet of pink lilies in one hand and Jonah's hand in the other. Haysleigh asked her to be her maid of honor. I'm so glad that they made up. Watching them throw away sixteen years of friendship over some bullshit revenge grudge almost broke me in two.

Now I get to enjoy both of my girls without having to worry about them killing each other.

We settle in front of the priest, and I'm having a hard time letting go of Haysleigh's shaking hand. For years, she's been only my girl, now I'm going to have to share her with another man that loves her just as much as I do.

"Who gives this woman away?" The priest asks me.

I turn toward my daughter and push a strand of her long brown hair out of her face.

V. Kelly

"Amelia, her brother, and I do," I remark, before kissing Haysleigh on the cheek.

Sonny reaches out for her hand, and I reluctantly give it to him. As a father, it kills me to give my daughter away, but I see the love shining in his eyes, it's the same look I get every time I look at my wife.

My eyes drift over to Amelia. She's six months pregnant with our next child. I've never seen anyone that looks as beautiful as she does pregnant. She always seems to be glowing. Yes, I know that sounds cliché, but she truly glows when she's expecting, almost like she's basking in her pregnancy like it's a ray of light. I promised her at least one more child after we had Jonah. When we found she was pregnant again, she decided that two was enough for us, and I couldn't agree more.

I make my way to the front row and sit down. Jonah immediately races to my side, snuggling up against me. He doesn't like to stand for too long because he gets bored easily.

As the priest begins the ceremony, my eyes can't help wandering over to my beautiful bride again. She sees me staring at her and mouths the words "I love you" to me.

I mouth "I love you" back before turning my attention back on Haysleigh. This time I can't hold back my tears.

My life changed after Haysleigh was born. I never expected to become a father at sixteen, but I never let that stop me from loving her. Even when things got rocky between us, my love for my daughter never stopped. I'm proud of the woman she's become. Sonny evens her out and has helped her mature into the amazing person she is now. She's learned a lot about forgiveness and understanding, and I feel like that's a big part of what helped her accept my relationship with Amelia.

Her acceptance was the only thing we needed to make this family complete, and now that we have it, our family finally feels whole.

V. Kelly

The End

But make sure you keep an eye out for
Finn's book:
His Little Intern (a naughty office romance)
and
Scott's book:
His Little Sister (a stepbrother romance)
Both will be coming out soon.

Also, if you haven't read Chase's controversial book, *His Little Cheater*, it's available in KU and on Amazon for only .99 cents.

Acknowledgements

Before I start acknowledging the people who helped make this book special, I'd like to let people know how much this book has meant to me.

Two and a half years ago I received the devastating news that my daughter has leukemia. For almost three years, I haven't been able to write like I've wanted to, mainly because I wasn't in the right headspace to write anything. During that time, I wrote one of my darkest books, His Little Cheater. That book needed to be written because at the time, I needed to write something that felt real. I received so much backlash for the way the book was written that there were times I felt like giving up on writing altogether. My sales plummeted. My will to write was but a distant memory. I had to find myself again, and that wasn't easy. So, there are quite a few people who kept me motivated and going during this dark time that I'd like to thank.

My Husband, the man who's always been my rock when I needed something sturdy to hold on to. Even when it felt like life was nothing but chaos, you've always been the constant staple that holds me together. I love you so much and love this family we have created with each other.

My Kids, I know these past few years have been incredibly difficult for our family, but I want to say that I love you both very much and I'm so thankful that I was blessed with such wonderful kids. I know that illness has kept you guys down, but you're both starting to get better and there is light at the end of the rainbow. You both are stronger than you think you are and have been incredibly patient with me even when I have mood swings. I love you both to the moon and back.

Annelise, God, what I wouldn't do without you, woman. Not only do I consider you my author BFF, and one of my best friends, but you've also been a strong friend to lean on every time I needed someone to talk to. You never turned your back on me, and were always there for me, even when your life was chaotic, during my time of turmoil. Words seem insignificant, because they can't be used to explain how much your support and friendship has meant to me. I love you.

Jessica, (Yes, she's my inspiration for Nurse Jessica), I want to thank you for encouraging me to keep writing even though I felt like I couldn't. We didn't talk every day, but the talks we did have were encouraging and kept me motivated. Thank you for sending me that book that helped me get over my writer's block. It was exactly what I needed to get back into writing. I also want to tell you how much your friendship means to me. You and Marty are like family to us, and our family is so thankful for everything you've done for us. Especially my daughter, who now considers you her honorary aunt and uncle.

K Webster, we don't really know each other, but your book *Paused to Prolific* really helped me break out of my shell and inspired me to finish this book. It was after reading your book that I started writing like a mad woman again. This book was only halfway done at the start of the year, and I barely touched it. Within two months after reading your book, I had it finished, and it was because your book helped me round up all the squirrels trying to distract my writing. So, thank you for writing a book that has helped and inspired me in so many ways.

Kate, you've been one of my best friends since we were in Kindergarten. There were times we drifted apart, but we always managed to find our way back to each other. I'm so thankful to call you and Devon family. Your friendship has meant the world to our family, and during this dark time, you were one of the few people who stuck by our side. I luffs you and want to thank you for always being there for me when I need you.

As always, I would like to thank my **readers** for sticking by my side even when I wasn't writing much. Your support means everything to me, and I'm hoping to get out more books this year so that you can read them. I love you all.

Laugh, Love, & Write

V. Kelly

His Little Cheater

By V. Kelly

A Forbidden Love Affair Series: Book One

(A Hot for teacher anti-romance)

Synopsis:

I've never considered myself the cheating type, but desperate times call for desperate measures, when your roommate throws a class ten kegger the night before your geometry midterm.

I didn't get in the amount of studying I had planned, and if it weren't for the fact that my hot as hell geometry teacher is a complete asshole, I wouldn't even be in this situation. But here I am, on all fours, with the test answers in hand, hiding underneath his desk, praying to God that he doesn't sit down and catch me.

You'd think a girl like me would be worrying about her future if she gets caught cheating, but as Professor Hanson sits down and his hand starts slowly rubbing the bulge in his tight jeans, I realize there's a lot more to him than I thought. ESPECIALLY when I hear him whisper MY name while touching himself. Now my future is the last thing on my mind.

WARNING

If you're looking for a story that follows the typical romance guidelines, this isn't it. It's hot, it's edgy... it's actually anti-romance. You won't like the leading man, you'll probably scream at the heroine, and it has an ending you won't see coming. This book is meant to make you think and redefine your typical erotic read. Contains a non-traditional happily ever after.

Want to Read more from V. Kelly?

Check out her other hilarious books and steamy reads.

To Be With You Series:

Book 1: *First Impressions*

It Had 2 B U Series:

Book 1: *Innuendos*
Book 2: *Accent Hussy* (Her POV)

Spinoff series Jacob's Gloves:

Caleb-Unaccented Pain in the Ass (His POV of Accent Hussy)

Pop! Duet:

Book 1: *Pop!*
Book 2: *Popped!*

Montgomery Ranch Series:

Book 1: *Just A Little Bit Country*
Book 2: *Just A little Bit Rock 'N' Roll*

Standalones:

Wooing the Witch

Jack Got Jilled

About the Author

V. Kelly grew up in Reno, Nevada, but now lives in Oklahoma, with her husband and two beautiful kids. Always a writer, it was only a matter of time before the stories in her head escaped and became available for the world to read. She is a lover of frogs, otters, all things green, reading books about compelling relationships, and spending time with her family.

If you like this story, please leave me a review on Goodreads or Amazon! Every review helps.

You can find her on Facebook at:

https://www.facebook.com/vkellyauthor?fref=ts

Visit her website:

www.vkellyauthor.com

Join her mailing list:

https://docs.google.com/forms/d/17Xg6Ykvw2x3YoL-zA3ZfUjavvn497ZaLKB2F9SqBh0M/viewform

Join her street team!

https://www.facebook.com/groups/vkellyskeepers/

You can follow her on Twitter at

https://twitter.com/VanessaFKelly

Or you can always email her at vkellyauthor@gmail.com